The
Carefully
Planned Move

Robert C. Stewart

Robert C. Stewart

The Carefully Planned Move

TO

Mother, PAT, Connie, Claire & Robert

Robert C. Stewart

CHAPTER ONE

Simon Chang sat in his rocking chair, looking out of the picture window of his second floor apartment. He had a view of the houses stacked next to each other across the street. They were old Victorian style buildings that had been split up and made into apartments that rented for $1700 per month and up. They were typical of San Francisco. He watched the foot traffic below as he rocked back and forth. He saw nothing of interest. At 2:30 PM he saw all the kids, mostly Chinese, leaving George Washington High School and he shrugged. They were teasing each other, yelling obscenities and laughing. He had had enough. He got up and walked to the back room, away from the noises of the street.

"Those kids have no respect for the people who have to live here."

He turned, expecting a comment and remembered that he was alone. His wife, Chi Mei, had gone shopping and Mary was never around. He shook his head when he thought about his daughter, Mary.

"She's a waitress with a college degree," he thought to himself, thoroughly disgusted.

As disapproving as he was, Simon was careful to never openly question his daughter's life choices. He left that chore to his wife. They had a mother and daughter relationship that could withstand an occasional shouting match. Many of their arguments were brutal. An outsider would swear that the things that were said between them would result in a rift that could never be repaired. But after a few days of the silent treatment, they were again poking fun at each other as if nothing had ever happened. Simon, on the other hand, was sure that even one snide remark from him would crush his daughter and irrevocably damage their relationship.

He was tormented by Mary's situation because she had so much potential and she wasn't doing anything with her life. He knew that if she put her mind to it, she could do almost anything. She could read people like a book, a children's book. Ten minutes after meeting someone, she could tell you what motivated them, what frightened them and what they cared most about. She instinctively knew how to manipulate people. It was an excellent skill for her to have. Simon had taught her everything else she needed to know and she was a good student. So many things came naturally to her.

"And now, she uses those skills to get good tips at a restaurant on Fisherman's Wharf."

He sulked for a few minutes and walked from room to room. He quickly figured out that it wasn't the noise of the children leaving school that upset him so much, nor was it Mary's life. He realized that he was tired of the monotony of doing nothing. He had enjoyed a successful career in the service of his country and now he was retired. For the last eighteen months, he had done nothing useful. He no longer had a purpose other than managing his portfolio. Watching the stock market go up and down and seeing his money grow or dwindle wasn't as exciting for him as his time on the job had been.

The job he loved and did for twenty-four years was developing assets and obtaining information for the People's Republic of China. The information that he and his handlers sought was proprietary intellectual property and Silicon Valley was a gold mine. As an intelligence agent, Simon Chang was aware that information in the right hands at the right time in the right place was invaluable. Sometimes, the right hands were his superiors in Beijing. Other times the right hands were his stock broker and money manager. The right time was the early 1990's and the right place was here in Northern California.

Simon did very well obtaining information that was of interest to the Chinese and his superiors were very happy with him. At the same time, he ran across information that provided insight into the health and potential of many of the start-up companies that sprang up like weeds in Mountain View, Sunnyvale and San Jose. Many of the companies were operating and developing products and services long before they had the proper security measures in place.

Simon's success came as a result of his ability to find and recruit his assets, and they were everywhere. He found the disgruntled employee who had just gotten passed over for a promotion and was more than happy to sell him his company's secrets. There were also the people he was able to blackmail by finding their weaknesses or documenting their indiscretions. But Simon got the bulk of his information from what he liked to call 'the cloaked people'. They were the people you didn't notice or you saw but quickly forgot. He recruited file clerks, janitors, and security guards. He recruited realtors and found out who made sales to executives who bought their new homes for cash. He also had clerks who were employed by many of the surrounding cities who were in a position to know which companies had filed for construction permits. Simon's network was extensive and expensive, but his information was good and his investment profits were enormous.

When the dot com bubble finally burst, Simon's contacts were just as valuable as ever. He was able to find out which companies were failing in which time frames. He sold their stocks short and made even more money. His financial contacts helped him form an off-shore shell company to hide and launder his money, and he avoided paying taxes for anything other than his modest salary as a medical equipment salesman. Simon was well off, but he and his family lived modestly and his daughter was never told of the family's money.

Simon and his wife were comfortable and they wanted Mary to grow up with good values and a good work ethic. This country had corrupted her enough with its decadent ideas and vulgar entertainment media and music. They didn't want her to be corrupted even further by the family having money. Instead, Simon let Mary believe that meeting their financial commitments each month was a struggle, and paying for her education was an amazing feat that her father had somehow managed to accomplish.

It seemed to have worked. Mary was grateful for everything she had. She worked hard and graduated from San Francisco State with honors. She found a job as a business trainee in an insurance office but quit after a month. Her explanation for quitting was that she wasn't interested in the insurance business and she wanted to take some time to discover what she wanted to do with her life.

She hung around the apartment for three months doing nothing, and then she found a job as a part-time waitress. At home, she argued with her mother constantly, forcing Simon to give her some work to do just to get her out of the apartment. He gave her work as a courier, traveling back and forth across the country. When Simon retired there was no more courier work for her and she started waitressing full time.

Simon went to his desk and turned on his computer to check his email. His machine was six years old and he had no plans to upgrade. Without it he couldn't have built or maintained his information network. Most of his sources were gone now, but occasionally people still sent him messages that they thought would interest him.

CHAPTER TWO

"Think about it, it's perfect. The board has been discussing it for weeks." Bob Watson leaned back in his plush chair and smiled smugly.

"I can't believe it. And they want me to spearhead the move?"

"Well, that part hasn't been settled yet. But you would be the natural choice. You speak the language, your grandparents emigrated from there, and your star is rising in the corporation. It's also no secret that a few of the top executives want you out of the way before you're given one of their spots."

"This is great news." Eric Wing was thrilled. He had worked for Universal Technology Systems for eight years. He had joined the company right out of grad school. He had earned four promotions, propelling him into the upper management ranks faster than any other employee.

"I'm only telling you this so that you'll be ready if and when they spring this on you. It's a big deal and I don't want you to be caught off guard."

"'Big deal', that's an understatement. A move to China would be the biggest thing the company has done since I've been here."

"Think about it and decide if you really want to do it. It would be a multi-year commitment and you'd be away from headquarters. It's not easy to impress the senior executives remotely. If you decide you're interested, start schmoozing the right people and preparing your acceptance speech. "

They both laughed, and Eric left Bob's office with his head spinning. He walked back to his office and plopped down exhausted in his desk chair. Eric quickly decided that Bob was right. If they were going to staff the position from within the company, he was the logical choice. Eric had headed the Manufacturing Division's western regional operation for eighteen months. The reason for going to China would be to set up a manufacturing operation.

"President of China Manufacturing, Manufacturing President – China Operations, President China Operations", he couldn't decide which title suited him best. He wished he had someone he could confide in to talk to about this potentially life changing choice he was about to make. But not having a family or a serious personal relationship would work in his favor if he was going to leave the country long term.

He knew that he had no choice if he was going to stay with the company. If he was offered the job, he had to take it. You had to be an aggressive, go-getter type to advance on the job. That posture had served him well for the past eight years. If he turned down a position for advancement for which he was perfectly suited, he'd never get another offer for anything.

His language skills were a little rusty, but here in the bay area, there were several Chinese language TV stations and he could be speaking like a native in a few short weeks. As for schmoozing the right people, it was a waste of time. At this level of management, the old-timers didn't have any questions about Eric. To them, you are what you looked like. To them, Eric wasn't one of their kind. Eric had reached upper mid-level management and he wasn't going any further until the old bigots at the top died off. This China move was his only opportunity to advance.

Sometimes, he wondered why he had stayed with the company as long as he had. The promotions came quickly and the money was good, but he was still like an associate in a law firm. He worked all the time. He had no life. Eric was 28, 5 feet 11 inches tall and weighed 185 pounds. His hair was black and he had a square chin and a warm, pleasant smile which he used sparingly. Eric had not been engaged in a relationship since college. She had been a townie, not Chinese and when he'd graduated and moved on to grad school, which had consumed all of his time, the relationship faded.

He thought China might be a new beginning without having to start all over from scratch. He might even meet someone new. Not that he couldn't find a nice Chinese girl here in San Francisco, but if you closed your eyes while talking to one of the girls from here, you'd swear you were talking to a blue-eyed, blond-haired valley girl.

Eric wasn't even sure what he would do with a life. He had no patience with women or men in social situations. His life pattern was to learn everything he could and use everything he learned. To him life was just a competition, a contest to find out who was the best. The workplace was his arena and he loved to win. He played fair, but he played to win.

His meeting with Bob was the last item on today's agenda, but he had planned to hang around and review monthly production reports. After Bob dropped the China bomb, he decided to run over to Larkin Street to the public library and pick up a few books about expanding your business to China. He had heard about the difficulties of working in foreign countries. He didn't think it was a good idea that the company's first international experience was going to be with the Chinese.

There had been rumors that something big was happening soon at Universal. The guys who delivered the mail were, as usual, on the lookout for any juicy bit of inside information they could sell to the media. Well, their buyers told them that they were with the media. In truth, most of them were day-traders who made out pretty well on the few points that Universal rose or dipped each business day.

Danny Long had worked in the mailroom for two years before he was promoted to Section Chief, responsible for mail pick-up and delivery. He hadn't wasted any time setting up a network of information gathering that would have made the BBC proud. Danny got the mail delivery guys to share any information they came up with. He also cultivated the senior secretarial staff to share information by providing them with pastries and thoughtful small gifts on the proper occasions.

All the information Danny received was passed on daily to his group of day-traders and to an independent business news gathering service, which in turn sold it to representatives of brokerage houses, news-outlets, business consultants, and anyone interested. There was a Danny Long at each major multi-national technology company in the bay area.

Today, Danny's information network confirmed that United Technology Systems was planning to move a major portion of its manufacturing operations to China and that Eric Wing was going to be responsible for the move. Shortly after Eric left Bob's office, that information was on its way to Beijing.

Eric left the building in daylight for the first time in years. He decided to walk to the library. It was foggy and chilly, good walking weather. The main library was only seven blocks from the O'Farrell Street office. He remembered that he liked the city back when he had time for it. He walked by the Asian Art Museum and was tempted to go in. Instead he continued on to 100 Larkin Street and found some books on the subject of doing business in China; there were a couple of "dummy" books. He picked up three introductory level books and found a couple of videos from the library's less than adequate collection.

He wasn't surprised that he had to renew his card. Fortunately he was able to do it on the spot, and he headed home.

Eric stayed up most of the night watching the videos and reading the borrowed books. The task of expanding to China grew more and more enormous with every new piece of information he learned. It was obvious that the company was going to need a lot of help.

He thought about raiding talent from companies that had already made the move to China. But he decided that it would be better to work with a consulting company specializing in doing business there. The down side of bringing in a consulting company was that the senior executives might think that they didn't need him. They might think that any manager would do. It didn't matter; Eric knew he couldn't do it by himself.

Back in the office, Eric was showing the effects of the nearly all-nighter. He was bleary-eyed. His secretary, Angel Davis, commented on his appearance. Angel was always constructive in her criticisms and he paid attention to whatever she said. She was his ally and loyal supporter. As he moved up the promotional ladder, he took her along with him and she returned the favor with fierce loyalty.

Angel was an angel. She was black and truly beautiful. She was five feet six inches tall and she weighed 128 pounds. Her proportions were perfect and her smile could make you forget your name. She was also smart, skilled and professional. There had been rumors in the office that there might be something personal going on between Eric and Angel, but it wasn't true.

Angel made Eric a cup of tea and he settled into his regular work routine. The China thing was a big distraction, but he soon got back to concentrating on his current responsibilities.

As he went through his day, Eric noticed the looks and glances he was getting from his peers. It didn't start with his peers; the mail room guy was the first person who looked at him with a silly grin. Then it was the upper management secretaries and then his peers. *"They know,"* he thought to himself. *"They all know."*

When he made it back to his office after a three hour meeting, Angel told him that the rumor was that he had been chosen to head up the move to China. She wasn't happy when she found out. She realized that their joint rise to the top was over. "You know that you don't have a choice. You'll have to take it when they offer it to you."

"I know, it's an opportunity of a lifetime. Fortunately, I don't have a life outside of the company, so it's not a big deal personally."

"I'll miss working for you. I hope they can place me with someone else with something on the ball."

Eric didn't even pretend there was a chance that Angel would be going to China with him. The company would never go for it and they could easily find someone there who not only spoke the language, but would not need relocation expenses and whose salary would be a lot less.

"I'll make sure you're taken care of," Eric said, hoping that Angel hadn't made too many enemies when she was promoted over the other secretaries during the last eight years.

She handed him a memo requesting his presence in the office of the chairman at 9:00 AM the next morning. "Be careful, this great opportunity might come with an unrealistic timetable and a handpicked team that is impossible to work with," said Angel, with a grim look. "It may not be a done deal yet."

He could understand her mixed feelings and took note of her warning. He watched her as she left the office and went back to her desk. He knew he wasn't going to get any work done the rest of the day, so he closed his eyes and tried to imagine what life was going to be like for the next few years. There would be so much to learn and so many obstacles to overcome.

It seemed like he had daydreamed for a few minutes, but when he looked at the clock, it was an hour past quitting time. Angel hadn't ducked her head in to say goodnight before she left, as was her usual practice. Eric packed his briefcase. He picked up the phone and called his barber to check on the wait time if he went directly to the shop. He decided that twenty minutes was an acceptable wait time and he headed out.

The rumor of the China move spread openly around headquarters. Don Baker and Steve Gross had anticipated an international move for some time, but they didn't expect that it would be China. As Eastern and Central Manufacturing Regional Managers, they had expected to be given a shot at the international job. But they expected the move would be to an English speaking country initially, and then after the company had gained some international expansion experience, they might make a move to a country like China.

Don and Steve had been in their current positions for six and eight years respectively. Years ago, they had figured out that company expansion was their only path up the promotional ladder. Now that Eric was going to be named to the new position, they realized that they would never advance any further. It would take years for the China move to be completed and even more time to determine whether it was a success or not. Their only hope was that Eric would fail and fail quickly, or that one or more of the company officers died.

Don and Steve had been friends since their undergraduate years at Fordham. They liked and respected each other, but they both knew that they'd cut one another off at the knees if there was a chance to get ahead in the company.

There were four Vice Presidents, one for each of the divisions: Manufacturing; Research and Development; Engineering and Installation; and Operational Services. Manufacturing was the largest and most costly division. It was inevitable that some manufacturing would be outsourced, but the board of directors wanted the Chinese people to be consumers of Universal Technology's products and services as well as producers. The move was an international public relations operation as well as a business strategy.

The plan was to double the company sales of robotic manufacturing equipment within five years. The move would be complicated by the fact that Universal also developed and built highly sensitive technological equipment for sale to the US government. The China operation would not be involved in the manufacturing of the high tech product line.

Both Don and Steve would have jumped at the China job if it was offered, but they also knew it was going to be next to impossible to pull off. They anticipated that the lucky stiff who got the job would work himself to death for two or three years, trying to get the job done. Upper management would tire of the missed deadlines and mounting expense, and just before the work was completed, he would be replaced by someone new who would get all the credit.

Since there was still a remote possibility that he might be their boss someday, Don and Steve were prepared to be the first ones in line to congratulate Eric when the time came.

Eric had a good night's sleep and was well-rested when he arrived at the office for what was to be the biggest day of his career. As expected, Angel was not in a good mood. She made his tea and gave him his messages and reminded him of his meeting at nine o'clock. Eric smiled and tried to focus on work for the hour he had before the meeting. He couldn't. He wasn't nervous, but he knew that this could easily be his last assignment with the company. 'High risk, high reward' accurately described this new work effort. He shuffled papers around until it was time to go, and then he rode the elevator to the top floor.

Eric was looking forward to meeting with the chairman. The chairman, Ralph Petersen, had started with the company at the age of fifteen. He was fired a year later when his supervisor found out that he had lied about his age when he was hired. He joined the Army and was rehired after his discharge. At that time, the company made furniture. Ralph worked as an assembler, went to school nights and slowly rose to the top. He was married for fourteen years and got divorced after his son was killed in a traffic accident. He devoted the rest of his life to the company. He was sixty-five and had no plans to ever step down.

The chairman's office was at the end of the hall on the twenty-third floor. The double doors opened to a large tastefully decorated office that had relatively few personal items displayed. There was a picture of the chairman shaking hands with President Bush, the first one. There was also a picture of a yacht in San Francisco Bay. There were no family pictures. The chairman always said that the company was his family. Behind a huge mahogany desk sat a gray-haired man who looked to be in pretty good shape. He stood and came around the desk and extended his hand. "Good morning, I'm Ralph Petersen," he said as he shook Eric's hand. "I've seen you around, and I've heard good things about you, but I don't believe we've ever talked before."

"No, sir, we haven't. It's good to finally meet with you."

"Have a seat. Of course, you know Bob Watson."

Eric looked in the direction of the chairman's gesture and he saw Bob Watson, the Vice President of Manufacturing. He didn't know how he'd missed seeing him. He didn't want to start the meeting off by slighting his boss. "Good morning, Bob. Good to see you."

Watson nodded in Eric's direction and turned to Ralph who continued speaking. "I suspect you already know why you're here, Eric, but I have to make it official. If you're willing to take on the responsibility, you will be named to head our China expansion project. You will report to Mike

Fowler, so this will be a promotion and will include a twenty percent bump in salary. You can meet with Mike later to discuss all the details. What do you say? Do you want the job?"

"Absolutely. Thank you, sir. Thank you very much."

"Good. We're going to announce your promotion in the auditorium at ten o'clock. Good luck."

With that, the chairman ushered Eric and Bob out of his office.

"I'm sorry I didn't acknowledge you when I came in the office, but my head hasn't been straight since you told me about the move." Eric was sincerely apologetic.

"Don't worry about it; I knew you were going to be in a daze. But now you've got to get over it and get ready to get to work."

"I know. You told me that the board had been discussing the move for weeks. Did they come up with any written proposal or guidelines or plan on how to proceed with the project?"

"Nothing usable. If you like, I can get the division heads together to pound out a strategy."

"That would be great as long as I'm not forced to adopt the strategy they come up with. I'm leaning toward hiring a consulting firm that specializes in helping businesses enter the Chinese market and establish working relationships with the Chinese government."

"That sounds like a good idea, but your first stop should be downstairs in Administrative Services. They need to clear the move with our own government. You'll need to help them share our plans with Washington and find out if they have any objections to our China move, and if so, what obstacles they're going to throw at us."

"I hope this project doesn't kill me."

"It might, but for now, we've got the meeting in the auditorium to announce your promotion and sing your praises. Enjoy it while you can."

There were almost fifty managers and support staff in the auditorium. These promotion announcements didn't happen often, but the format was always the same. The newly promoted employee's boss would give a brief talk about the employee and his accomplishments. Then he'd introduce the employee who would say how much he enjoyed working at the company and how grateful he was for the opportunities he had been given. After the applause, everyone would go to the tables in the rear of the auditorium for refreshments.

This gathering didn't go as expected. When everyone was finally seated and ready to begin, the Chairman walked in and took the podium. He welcomed everyone and began to talk about the Board of Directors' decision to expand the manufacturing operation to China. He emphasized the importance of the move and the plan to sell the products made in China to the vast market there. Then he described the board's search for someone to lead the project. He said that the board had settled on Eric Wing. For the next twenty minutes he talked in detail about Eric's accomplishments. He talked about Eric's successes as if he had taken part in every project. The Chairman's enthusiasm about the move to China and Eric left little doubt that both had his full support. The Chairman's other message also came through loud and clear; if anyone did anything to sabotage the project, they'd have hell to pay.

Eric listened to the speech and he couldn't believe that the man who barely gave him three minutes of his time half hour ago could now give him such a glowing tribute and his unqualified support in front of the whole company. "That crafty old fox," Eric said to Bob, sitting to his left. "Now he knows I'll make this project work or die trying."

The handshaking and backslapping went on for half an hour and people who had never spoken to him before congratulated him and seemed genuinely happy for him. Even Don Baker and Steve Gross pledged their support. Eric did have one concern; the president of the company, Mike Fowler, was nowhere to be found. It was very unusual for a manager to not be on hand to welcome a new direct reporting employee.

Eric's promotion had changed the company's organization chart. In the new structure, Bob Watson's title changed from "Vice President of Manufacturing" to "Vice President of Manufacturing, North America". Eric's title was now "Vice President of Manufacturing, International". Eric reported directly to Mike Fowler, President, Universal Technology Systems.

Eric followed Bob back to his office to discuss the details of his new job and the compensation that he'd receive as a result of his promotion to the ranks of upper management. "I noticed that Mike Fowler wasn't at the ceremony. Is there a problem?"

"Mike wasn't totally on board with the move to China."

"Shit! Why didn't you tell me this before?" Eric was pissed.

"Would it have made any difference?"

"Yes. It would have given me a clearer picture of what I was getting myself into."

"Eric, you weren't going to change your mind about accepting the job no matter who wasn't on board," Bob said confidently. "If I'd thought for a moment that you'd turn it down, I would have told you everything."

"You're right. There was no way I was going to turn it down. But now that I'm in all the way, suppose you tell me everything I need to know."

"I didn't hold out much, just that Mike was strongly against it. He thought it was too ambitious for us to go to China first. He also had a problem with the sensitive nature of the company's business and the fact that China has been caught spying against our country."

"Those are legitimate concerns."

"But it wasn't enough to deter the board. They steamrolled him. The board said the profit potential was too great to ignore and that we would take the necessary steps to safeguard our technology. They were also sure that if the project was approved, our government would provide enough oversight to prevent any problems."

Eric was aware of the news reports of spying on the part of the Chinese in order to get their hands on all types of western technology from biomedical to military. *"But the Chinese are not our enemies,"* he thought to himself. *"They're just our very aggressive friends."*

CHAPTER THREE

Before the Wall Street Journal could publish the news of Eric Wing's promotion, word had gotten to the Office of Business Operations (OBO) in Beijing. Universal Technology Systems had been a company of interest for several years. Individuals had been assigned to become familiar with the company's operations, organizational structure and product line.

The OBO was housed in a large office building in the heart of the city. The office employed 1500 people at this location with the mission of tracking companies with desirable technology and/or intellectual property. Employees monitored news broadcasts, financial markets, and business publications.

The OBO had employees in the countries where targeted companies were located. These on-site employees were, in some cases, employed by the targeted company. In other situations, OBO employees positioned themselves close to targeted company employees. In the United States, the OBO funded several firms that provided consulting services for companies interested in expanding to China. The OBO was not part of the Chinese government, but it was funded by the Chinese military, the Office of Agriculture and several other branches of government.

OBO field employees were trained in the languages and customs of foreign countries, international business, psychology, fashion, self defense and many other disciplines. Some OBO employees had never been to China, having been born in foreign countries and literally grandfathered into the OBO.

Over the years, the OBO provided extremely valuable technological information to the interested agencies, leading to important gains for the government. The OBO provided reports to the various government agencies on a daily basis.

The work that Universal Technology Systems did in the area of robotics was of great interest, as was the software work being done for the US Military.

Dr. Jiang Wang was the head of the OBO. Dr. Wang's background was in Nuclear Physics. He was 54 years old. He had graduated from the People's University of Beijing at 21 and stayed on to teach. He had taught for six years and was then recruited into the country's Nuclear Development Program. Dr. Wang had distinguished himself among his peers and superiors in the program. He was frustrated and outspoken about China's trailing the West in technological innovations. He had advocated a sharing of technology among developing and under-developed countries. If a country had access to technology that would increase crop yield or help provide clean water, he believed that it should be shared. He thought that medical innovations should also be shared. If compensation was required, he believed that the developing country could provide IOUs to the donor country that could be cashed in when the developing country was more stable and better able to pay its debts.

He was quickly educated to the fact that countries were primarily interested in their own advancement. If all they got for their generosity was the promise that someday they might be repaid, they wouldn't participate. He concluded that if China were strong enough, it could implement humanitarian technology sharing. He also concluded that it was easier and quicker to acquire technology than it was to develop it.

Dr. Wang applied for and accepted a position in the OBO as an evaluator of newly acquired technical properties. In his new position, Dr. Wang and his group of one hundred and forty well-educated individuals were responsible for incorporating the newly acquired technical property into an existing active project, or initiating a new project if the property had the potential for creating a new product, system or service. In this position, Dr. Wang was familiar with all project activities. He was briefed regularly on all weapon systems, toxins, guidance systems, propulsion systems, power systems, storage systems, etc., being developed in China. In addition to evaluating technological property, Dr. Wang and his group also developed lists of items that were targeted for retrieval. Dr. Wang held his position as Head of Property Evaluation for fourteen years before being made Head of the OBO.

The United States was the country that the OBO concentrated on most. The OBO had major operations in Boston, MA; Herndon, VA; Dallas, TX; and San Francisco, CA. The OBO had a three person team in the San Francisco bay area which monitored and controlled the fifty-four assets located there. Internet Startups were the responsibility of Hu Peng. The major corporations in the area were split between Hui Kai and Ma Qishan. United Technology Systems was one of Hui Kai's companies.

Hui Kai was elated when he heard that Eric Wing had been named as Vice President of UTS with the mission of expanding to China. Hui had seen Eric Wing's dossier and he wasn't sure if Eric was a good candidate to be recruited or corrupted. According to the information available, Wing had no vices and he was not in a relationship. Hui had to look into the possibility that he might be gay; after all, he was in San Francisco. If he was gay, that would also be good news.

Hui Kai prided himself on the selection and control of his assets. He was a small man, both in stature and intellectual flexibility. Hui was fifty-seven with a medium build except for his shoulders which were square and slightly bigger than normal for his frame. His jet black hair was thick and unruly and looked like he was past due for a trip to the barber. His bushy eyebrows were a distraction and an observer would usually not notice the cruelty in his brown eyes.

He had one opinion of the people he worked with. Hui always assumed that whomever he was dealing with was devious, self-serving and untrustworthy. His views had served him well for the twenty-four years he had spent as a handler. No one had held the job as long as he, a fact that his wife would point out whenever she wanted to wound him. Hui's success at his job, which was the way he chose to look at it, was due to his ability to use intimidation and fear, when necessary, to manage his assets.

Hui was familiar with the list of assets in Northern California, but he reviewed it anyway. He started his computer and connected to the OBO mainframe, which changed its IP address to a machine's located in Perth, Australia. Hui got on-line and sent a message to Mary Chang telling her to check her Union Square Post Office Box as soon as possible.

Hui had arranged for a copy of Eric's dossier and $1500 to be sent to the Post Office Box. Mary Chang had been chosen to contact Eric because she had all the qualifications necessary to interest a single male. She was beautiful, smart and trained by her father, who before retiring was one of Hui's best operatives. Mary was a second generation American whose parents had served the Intelligence Services of China for over twenty years. They had trained their daughter to speak Chinese and embrace their philosophy. She had also been trained in psychology, the social graces and self defense. She had a bachelor's degree in Creative Arts with a minor in Psychology at San Francisco State. She was twenty-six years old, five feet seven, with a slender build.

Mary's parents had also taught her to be very careful. They taught her that there was a very real threat of jail time or worst if she was caught stealing company secrets. Being identified by the Commerce Security Agency for involvement in or supporting economic terrorism against the United States was a very serious matter. It was not commonly known, but the CSA had been authorized by a secret congressional subcommittee to use rendition techniques to combat any foreign interests involved in the theft of creative or intellectual property that resulted in significant economic loss.

Mary had four previous assignments that she handled successfully. Although she lived in San Francisco, she never worked in the bay area before. She traveled to New York, Atlanta, Washington D. C., and Houston for her other jobs. She had only been a courier, but she also did reconnaissance work. She had a remarkable memory for places and faces that was very useful.

Hui Kai, through his intermediaries, contacted the Montgomery Group and made them aware of UTS's plans for expansion. The Montgomery Group was a consulting company specializing in supporting American business ventures in and into Asia. Hui had several contacts in the Montgomery Group. The Montgomery contacts did not work for Hui, but they valued his insight and his counsel. They knew that he wasn't in the government, but he had demonstrated that he could facilitate business related projects. They were told to introduce themselves to Eric Wing at UTS and ask for an opportunity to make a presentation about their services.

Hui was aware that there was going to be opposition from US Government officials to the UTS expansion plans. He wanted to get his assets in Washington working to reduce or eliminate the resistance to the project. There were several lobbyists on the OBO payroll. The lobbyists had been successful before, pushing the idea that with the current economy, the US should do everything it could to expand to new markets. He understood that it would be months before the US Government would look at the UTS project, but he planned to be ready to combat any resistance when the time came.

Hui was sure that he had done all he could for the present. He wanted to be thorough. In Beijing, the monitors met weekly with the Head of Property Evaluation to review active projects, the current course of action and the progress on each project. If a monitor didn't cover every angle of his project, he would be openly humiliated at the meeting.

"What can I get for you?" said Mary sweetly as she stood by the table, pencil in hand, ready to take the couple's order. Mary Chang enjoyed her job waitressing. When she was hired, she had told her prospective boss that she was an actress who waited tables and if she got an acting job, the lunch crowd would have to wait. She was good at her job and her employer tolerated her occasional absences. The truth was that she had no interest in acting at all.

Mary was in the middle of the lunch rush. Her job allowed her to interact with a large number of people and since the restaurant was a tourist location, she dealt with people of different nationalities. Mary got a chance to practice her French and Italian. Her good looks made it easy to initiate little chats with the ladies. Her looks also made it necessary for her to fend off advances from the men, both young and old. Her skill and personality made her a customer favorite, resulting in excellent tips.

By two in the afternoon, the lunch crowd was gone and the restaurant had been set up for dinner. Mary had three and a half hours to herself before her next shift. She was able to make it home to her parents' place on Anza Street in twenty minutes. She stretched out on her bed for a minute and tried to figure out what she was going to do after work. She hadn't been with a man in weeks and she thought about maybe accepting one of the many offers she got to go out on dates.

"Mary, are you hungry? Do you want something to eat?"

"I work in a restaurant, Ma. I eat all day long."

"You not answer my question."

"No, Ma, I'm not hungry. Thank you anyway."

"That better, answer me when I talk to you. I try to be nice and you answer nasty."

"Yes, Ma."

Mary knew her mother was angry when she resorted to broken English, so she didn't push her. The old lady had a problem expressing herself when she lost her temper. When she responded in Chinese, Mary knew her mother was furious.

Since her quiet time was disrupted, Mary got up, went to her desk and turned on her laptop. She read the e-mail from her handler. She thought about going to the post office right away, but decided to go after work. There was no rush since there was 24 hour access to the post office boxes.

She lay back down on her bed and wondered what her new assignment was going to be. She hoped they didn't ask her to do something she couldn't handle, like physically hurt someone. She had told her parents that she had mixed feelings about her work for the Chinese. She didn't think about it much, but she loved this country. She took it for granted like everybody else. Working for the Chinese was something her parents told her was the right thing to do, so she did it. It was like when your parents told you what religion you belonged to. You joined, you believed, but every so often, you had your doubts.

Mary napped until 4:45 PM and then headed back to work. She started paying attention to everything she saw on the bus ride back to the restaurant. There was a two year old boy sitting next to his mother across the aisle. He said "No!" to everything his mother said to him. The more he used his favorite word, the bigger his smile got. His mother kept talking and he kept saying "No!" like it was a contest to see who'd give up first. Thankfully, they reached their stop and got off. Mary turned her attention to an old lady who was wearing a handmade hat and scarf. They were not only handmade; they looked like they were homemade. She wore them proudly. When she saw Mary staring, she said, "My granddaughter made this hat and scarf. Aren't they lovely?" Mary had to agree.

Mary took in all she could about everyone on the bus. Then on the four block walk to work, she mentally photographed the buildings and people and cars. She even took note of the incline in the sidewalk on the streets. The new assignment had her concerned. She had a feeling that everything was about to change, and she wanted to remember how things were, before it was too late.

Mary worked the dinner shift; it seemed like the

longest shift she had ever worked. When it was over, she was exhausted. She just wanted to go straight home and sleep for as long as she could. Instead, Mary hopped on a bus going in the opposite direction, went to the post office box and retrieved a large envelope. She put it in her bag and walked back to the bus stop to go home.

It was after 10:00 PM when Mary flopped down on her bed and ripped open the envelope. She saw the dossier and the cash, and there was a type-written page with her instructions. It explained that the man described in the dossier was going to be responsible for expanding a branch of his large technical company to China. It said that her assignment was to meet and get close to this man. She was to get as close as possible.

Mary was shocked. She'd never prostituted herself before and she wasn't sure whether she'd do it this time either. She stopped and took a deep breath. She decided to take in all the facts before she made any assumptions or passed judgment on the assignment. As tired as she was, Mary read and studied the dossier until 2:20 AM.

When she finished reading, she was no longer concerned about having to sleep with Eric Wing; she didn't even believe that she would be able to meet him. The man was a monk. He didn't do anything but work. He didn't go clubbing, he had no church affiliation and no family. Mary decided that since she couldn't meet him socially, she would have to meet him on a professional basis. The dossier stated that the Montgomery Group would be contacting Mr. Wing to offer their services for the China move.

Mary turned on her laptop. She contacted a friend in New Orleans and told him that she had decided to apply for a job with the Montgomery Group and she would appreciate all the help she could get to secure a position. Mary indicated that the job she was applying for would put her in direct contact with the executives of the company's clients. Mary also told her friend that she would need at least ten thousand dollars to upgrade her wardrobe to dress appropriately for her new job. In addition to the new job, she was going to have to move to a new place. The apartment she had in mind was upscale and it was a place where young executives lived.

Mary smiled broadly when she shut down her computer. *"My virtue has a stiff price,"* she said to herself. She expected her assignment to be canceled or given to another asset. Mary felt relieved. She was still emotionally exhausted, but she was starting to relax.

She went to the kitchen and poured herself a glass of wine. Her parents were sleeping, so she put in her MP3 ear buds and listened to her favorite playlist. It was 4:00 AM when she woke up. She looked around and saw that she was in the living room on the couch. She got up and walked to the kitchen to put her wine glass in the sink. She yawned and stretched her arms on the way to her room. She fell on the bed and went back to sleep.

CHAPTER FOUR

"I've received introductory letters and brochures from three consulting firms," said Eric. "I suppose we should invite them all to meet with us and listen to their spiel."

"That sounds okay. But let's get them in here ASAP," Bob was acting as if it was his career that was on the line.

"Hey relax, we've got plenty of time," said Eric.

"I know how these things work. Before you know it, the board is asking for status reports and time charts. He may not have said anything, but the CEO has a timetable in his head. He'll share it with you after he decides you're behind schedule."

"I know, you're right. We'll find time next week to have them all in here."

Eric really appreciated how Bob had jumped in and supported him on the project. Eric needed someone to bounce ideas off and consult with, but he knew that it was his neck on the line and only his.

"I heard good things about the Montgomery Group, but I guess they're all the same," said Bob, preparing to leave for the day.

"One metric I want to hear is how long it took for their customers to get up and running in China. As far as I'm concerned, the consulting company who can tell me that they are the fastest facilitator gets my vote."

"It has been a long exciting week for you. Have a good

weekend." Bob gave Eric a half wave as he left. Eric sat back in his office chair and looked out of the window toward the bay. *"So far so good,"* he thought to himself. Eric planned to spend most of the weekend right there in the office documenting the status of his old responsibilities for whoever was taking his place.

Mary woke tired and a little groggy after her long night. But it was her day off and she wasn't going to waste it. She bounded out of bed and headed for the shower. She didn't have any plans, but she loved the city, and she thought she'd play tourist. She put on her jeans and a black, cotton shirt and her Nikes. She turned on her laptop and checked her mail. There was a new email message. It stated that she was going to meet a new man and she was going to get a new job, a new wardrobe and a new apartment. Her friend said that she was going to be with this man no matter what it took.

"Shit!" Mary said, more loudly than she intended.

"Did you say something, Mary?" called her father from the kitchen. The old man was reading the morning paper and having his tea.

"No, Dad, I didn't say anything. Just making noises."

"Mary, come and get your breakfast. It's ready." Her mother was in the kitchen too. They were both there, ready to ambush her. The only way for her parents to spend time with Mary, and find out what was going on in her life, was to wait for her to emerge on her day off and give her the third degree over breakfast. Mary walked into the kitchen. She was acutely aware of her parents' ritual.

"I don't want to talk this morning. I've got something

on my mind and I don't want to talk about it, okay."

"We only want to know what is going on with you."

"I know, Ma, but I don't want to talk about it now. Please let it go."

"Mary, your mother and I only want to help. Tell us what is troubling you."

"I've got an assignment! Now, can we stop talking?"

It was an unwritten rule that the family didn't talk about the work they did for China. Mary fully expected that admission of an assignment would end the conversation. It didn't. Regardless of how they treated her, Mary was everything to them; unwritten rules didn't matter.

"You've had assignments before, why does this one trouble you?"

"Because, this assignment calls for me to get close to a businessman. I interpret 'get close to' to mean sleep with. I don't want to prostitute myself."

Mary's mother put her hand over her mouth and let out a muffled sob. Her father lowered his head.

He looked up at Mary and said, "Maybe you could talk to your handler and tell him of your inexperience and suggest he use another asset."

"You know that won't work. I have to do it, or tell him no and face the consequences."

Mr. Chang looked at Mary and his wife and said, "Your mother and I will stand by any decision you make. We know that you have deep affection for this country and your commitment to China is not strong. We will stand with you. If we have to leave here and go into hiding, we will."

Mrs. Chang nodded her head in agreement.

"I have to be by myself and think about it. I love you both." Mary picked up her jacket and walked out.

Mary left her parents' apartment and walked to the top of the hill near the school and looked around. She saw the top of the bridge above the fog. Then she turned and walked back down the hill towards the ocean. She walked about four or five blocks and stopped. She hadn't decided anything. She hadn't thought about anything. What was she going to do? She was scared.

"*This is crazy,*" she thought to herself. "*It's not like I'm a virgin. And who knows, this is San Francisco, he might be gay. It's really not a big deal. I've done bad things before. I'm getting ahead of myself. I might even like the guy. Get it together, Mary. I've played guys before without having to close the deal. I need to chill.*"

She knew what she wasn't going to do. She wasn't going to force her parents to leave their home and go into hiding. She didn't want them to become an enemy of a world power that they couldn't successfully run or hide from. Even from her limited experience, she knew things that would interest the authorities. And who knows how many secrets her parents knew that could embarrass America's ally.

Mary turned the corner and walked to Balboa Street. She stopped at a little sweet shop and got an espresso and a muffin for breakfast. She had to go back home and tell her parents that she was going to accept the assignment before they packed and cleaned out their bank accounts.

Mary finished her breakfast and walked back home. She came in quietly. Her parents were still in the kitchen. She sat down and she said, "Mom and Dad, I really don't think I have a choice. I'm going to accept the assignment. I won't have you going into hiding and trying to run. It isn't fair to you. I agreed to work for them. I know I can't pick and choose what I will do and what I won't do. I'm going to honor my commitments."

"This isn't necessary, if we have to run, we'll run. I still know a few tricks," her father said reassuringly.

"I know you do. Maybe we'll need them later. But for now, I'll work the assignment and see where it takes me."

Mary hugged her parents, and her father said, "I'll take a few precautions just in case."

Mary went to her room and turned on her laptop. Another message told her to expect a package before the end of the month. That meant her instructions and support materials were waiting for her in the PO Box. She took a deep breath and stiffened herself like a soldier coming to attention. She put her laptop in its case and slipped out of the apartment without saying goodbye. She suspected that every goodbye would start her parents worrying.

She caught the bus going back toward Union Square. This time things were different. She didn't pay attention to anything going on around her. She concentrated on what she learned in her many psychology classes. She had to get close to a man. She hoped that the months she spent learning about human behavior would help her. Getting close could mean physically or emotionally or even just intellectually. She had male friends who were only interested in her mind. She could name two right off the top of her head. There were only two, and she suspected that they were bullshitting her. Most of her straight male friends were interested in her body and she knew it.

She almost missed her stop, but she came out of her trance in time. She walked to the Post Office almost in tears and opened the box. The package was there as she expected. Her handler and his people were reliable and professional. Mary thought about how unprofessional she was. She put the package in her bag and walked out.

She decided to stick with her original plan for the day. She was around the corner from the museum of modern art and about ten blocks from the cable car museum. She was going to be a tourist for a couple of hours, and then she'd get to work.

She tried to enjoy herself, but the thought that her world was about to change was with her every second. Mary finished playing tourist and returned home about 4:00 PM. It was exhausting. She climbed the stairs and entered the apartment and went to her room. Her parents were usually napping at this hour. She sat down on the bed and opened the package. She dumped the contents on the bed. There was a credit card, more money, a cell phone, a letter of instructions, a resume, a set of keys and some legal papers.

The papers were a lease for an apartment on Nob Hill. She recognized the address from Eric Wing's dossier; it was two blocks away from his apartment. The resume had her name on it. As she read it she smiled. She saw that there were a few changes in her life as described in the document. It said that she graduated from SF State with a major in international business, and her minor was in psychology. It stated that she had been employed by an east coast consulting firm for six years, rising to the level of Assistant Vice President.

She put aside the resume and looked at the instruction sheet. It was written in Chinese. She struggled at first, but then read it without too much effort. It told her to purchase a wardrobe befitting a mid-level executive and present herself to Mr. Tong of the Montgomery Group on Tuesday morning at 10:00 AM. She marveled at the power and reach of her handlers, and she assumed that the job interview with Mr. Tong was just a formality.

Mary reached in her bag and found her cell phone. She

called the restaurant and told her boss that she had accepted an acting job and that if all went well it would be months before she returned to work. She went over her resume in detail several times, and then she picked up the package contents and left to see her new apartment.

CHAPTER FIVE

Eric decided to start leaving work shortly after the regular workday ended. He didn't want it to appear that the job was going to be too much for him. He planned to do a lot of work at home to make it appear that he was taking the new job in stride. He was going to upgrade his home office and find and use every technological advantage he could. He wanted to have everything he needed right at his fingertips to do his job whether he was at home or in the office.

He made a list of everything he needed to do to upgrade his home office. He planned to lay out his requirements to the Information Technology guys at work and find out what mobile devices he needed. He started to rearrange the furniture to accommodate the new computers he was planning to get. Suddenly, he stopped and took a deep breath. It was Sunday and he needed to take a day off. He went to the kitchen, got a beer and turned on the early NFL game.

Eric forced himself to watch the game. He got up and stretched. He decided to take a long walk to help him loosen up and relax. He knew that if he got a little exercise at least he'd get a good night's sleep.

The air outside was clear and crisp. The fog had burned off and the temperature was 64 degrees. Good football weather. The Niners were at home against the Broncos and everyone was either at Candlestick or glued to their TV sets. Eric had the city to himself.

He walked for a couple of blocks and he passed a bus

stop as a bus was pulling up. One of the passengers getting off was a young woman about twenty-five or so with a nice figure and a pleasant face. Their eyes met and she quickly looked away and walked past him up the street. Eric wouldn't have given it another thought except for the way the young woman averted her gaze. It was like she recognized him for a second and then didn't want to be seen. Maybe he reminded her of someone she disliked. He turned and watched her walk away. She was wearing blue jeans and a green jacket. He walked past some of the many mom and pop storefront shops on the street. One that caught his eye was a computer repair shop. He thought about the meeting he wanted to set up with the IT guys the first thing Monday morning, and he forgot what the young woman's face looked like. She was just a blur in jeans and a green jacket. He walked for a few more blocks and she was completely gone from his memory.

"Shit!" said Mary audibly enough to turn heads as she walked. She recognized Eric from the picture in the dossier. She had turned her head and averted her eyes as quickly as she could, but that might have been suspicious enough to get his attention and cause him to remember the incident and the young woman he saw. She hoped she was being silly. No one remembered people they see for an instant on the street. If he did remember her, she had an explanation for being in the neighborhood; she lived there. However, she didn't have an explanation for acting like a nut case.

She continued up the street to the address on the lease. She fumbled with the keys and found the one that fit the outer door. Entering the hall, she half expected to see a uniformed security guard patrolling the building. The building was impressive, the walls and the floor were marble. There was an elevator at the end of the hall, but she opened the door labeled 'Stairway' and climbed the steps to the third floor. She found apartment 306 and used the remaining key to open the door.

The apartment was fully furnished. The furniture was antique and the size of the place was enormous. She marveled at the crown molding and high ceilings. She ran from room to room like a child looking in all directions. There were eight rooms and two and a half bathrooms. The rooms appeared to be freshly painted in colors that she might have chosen herself. The colors were muted and each room was a different color. All the walls in the apartment at home were white. This was a refreshing change. She ran to the kitchen and looked at all the appliances. The place was fabulous; it was just what she always wanted.

There was an envelope on the dining room table. She opened it to find the keys and registration for a 328i BMW. She had a car! There was probably a garage in the basement. She pulled the lease out of her bag and started reading it. It stated that there was a parking area assigned to the apartment, space six. She left the apartment and took the elevator to the basement. She found the door labeled 'Garage' and located a cream colored BMW in space six. It was two years old, but it looked to be in good condition. She fell in love with it before she opened the door and sat behind the wheel. She knew that driving in the city would be a nightmare, but now she was free to leave the city and drive north to the wine country or east to Reno or anywhere she wanted.

This was too good to be true. It came to her suddenly that there was a price attached to all these wonderful things she now possessed. She went back up to the apartment and curled up on the couch in the living room. She resisted the urge to feel sorry for herself and, at the same time, remembered that she alone put herself in this predicament.

She got up and looked over the place in detail. There was food in the refrigerator and cabinets, so there was no need to go grocery shopping. That would save her a little time. She did have to buy clothes, upscale but off the rack; she had no time for tailoring.

She heard the grandfather clock in the entrance hall chime that it was six o'clock. She went in the library and found a book on doing business in China. She wasn't surprised that it was there among the extensive business book collection. She took it to the master bedroom and tossed it on the bed. She knew she was in for a sleepless night anyway.

Eric arrived at the office early as usual, ready to chip away at the mountain of problems facing him. He laid out his requests to the IT Department and was told he'd have everything he wanted by the end of the week. His next task was to assure the bureaucrats in Washington that no technological secrets would be given to China. The conference call with Washington and the company lawyers took up most of the morning, but it was only step one in the process of pacifying the government. Eric ate lunch at his desk with his staff, bouncing around ideas. The entire staff quickly realized that they needed to choose and start working with an experienced consulting group to get the project started in the right direction.

After lunch, Eric returned a call he had gotten from the Montgomery Group. After the usual pleasantries, Bill Robinson, Regional Manager of the Montgomery Group, said that they would be happy to give an onsite presentation in two weeks. Eric expressed his desire to choose a consulting partner immediately and that waiting two weeks was unacceptable. Bill said he could pull together a generic presentation right away if Eric and his staff could come to Montgomery's offices. Since the offices were located six blocks away, the meeting was set for the next day at 11:00 AM.

It was 1:20 PM and Mary had been shopping all day. She had purchased ten outfits suitable for the office and three casual ones. She was tired and sick of shopping. The clothes had started looking alike, so she stopped and went back to the apartment to take a break and review what she bought. She wondered what the limit on the card was. She had spent nearly five thousand dollars. It would have been more, but she found undergarments in her size in the dresser drawers in the master bedroom. The price tags were still on the items. That discovery had added to her discomfort and contributed to her sleepless night. It seemed that every time she accepted her situation and was getting with the program, she was reminded of the price she was going to have to pay.

She'd had some happy moments during her shopping spree, but now she was sad again. She began to put away her new clothes, and her new cell phone rang. She answered it, "Hello."

"Hello, Miss Chang. This is Mr. Tong of the Montgomery Group."

"Yes, Mr. Tong, I'm looking forward to meeting with you tomorrow."

"Miss Chang, the reason I called is that we have a crisis of sorts in the office. Due to the volume of work we have, we're going to have to have our interview today. Can you come in at 4:00 PM?"

"Yes, sir, I can."

"Wonderful. I'm sure this interview is only a formality. Your resume is excellent and you come very highly recommended. But I'm getting ahead of myself. I'll see you at 4:00 PM. Ask for me at the guard station in the lobby."

"Yes, sir. Goodbye." She signed off the call and ran to the closet and looked at her new clothes. For this impromptu interview, she decided to go casual with a white silk blouse and dark brown pants. It was a little after two, and she needed twenty minutes travel time. She was too nervous to eat lunch, so she headed for the shower.

Mary arrived at the Montgomery Group's offices at 3:45 PM and as instructed, she asked for Mr. Tong at the guard station. She was given a badge and escorted upstairs to the tenth floor. Mr. Tong's office was large and modern. It was decorated with Chinese paintings and statuettes. As she stepped in the office, a small spry man, balding and fiftyish, got up and walked to her with his hand extended.

"Hello, Miss Chang, I'm Charles Tong. Welcome to the Montgomery Group."

"Thank you, Mr. Tong; it's a pleasure to meet you." Mary was directed to a guest chair next to the office's oversized desk.

"Please have a seat, Miss Chang. Thank you for coming on such short notice, but we are trying to take on a new client and we will be giving him a presentation tomorrow in the time slot I had scheduled for your interview." Mr. Tong walked behind the desk and sat down. "As I said in our brief phone conversation, your resume is excellent and you have been highly recommended. So, we would like you to join our team. We are staffing up in anticipation of landing the new client that I referred to. If we don't land the client, there is no need for the additional staff. Do you understand?"

"Yes, sir, perfectly."

"Good." He handed her an envelope. "There are the details of the job offer. The starting salary and benefits are laid out. It will take a few days to find and furnish an office for you. If you decide to take the job, I want you to attend the initial client presentation. The presentation is at 11:00 AM tomorrow; show up at ten and I'll introduce you to the rest of the team. On your way out, ask my secretary for a company orientation package. Do you have any questions?"

"No, sir, I don't."

"Good. If you think of anything you want to know, call me." He reached in his breast pocket and pulled out a business card and handed it to her. She didn't take it.

"Is this a test, Sir? Usually Chinese businessmen exchange cards using two hands."

"Yes it is," he said with a smile. He grasped the card with both hands and handed it to her. "I'll see you tomorrow morning at 10:00 AM."

She took the card and left the office, grateful that she had spent the night reading the book on doing business in China.

On the bus ride back to the apartment, she opened the envelope and read that her starting salary would be two hundred and fifty thousand dollars and she would have full medical and be included in the management stock option plan. "Too bad that it's only make-believe," she said to herself.

Eric had spent the rest of the work day trying to arrange to meet with two other consulting companies. Neither company was as flexible as the Montgomery Group. If the presentation went well, Eric would go with Montgomery and dump them later if things didn't work out.

It was past seven, two hours after the end of a normal work day. He'd try to leave on time tomorrow. He packed a couple of library books to read when he got home and he left. As he walked out, he noticed that the building was almost empty. He felt alone. He was tired of going home to an empty apartment.

The job, as exciting as it was, was no longer enough for him. He wanted to connect with someone. He really didn't know many women socially and he wasn't interested in any of the women he did know. Maybe Angel was the one exception, but she probably wouldn't be interested in him. He was contemplating joining an online dating site when he reached his bus stop.

The bus ride and the walk from the bus stop to his apartment did Eric a lot of good. The sights and sounds of the city distracted him and the fresh, cold air invigorated him. He was reminded that there was plenty of time left for him to meet someone and build a relationship. He was only twenty eight. There was plenty of time, but from now on, he wasn't going to waste any of it.

He decided it was time to put himself out there. He was going to make friends and find someone special. He was going to socialize. He was going to look at his socializing as just another work project in his life. He was going to create a project plan and work the plan.

He reached home and went directly to his den and

drew up a rough project plan to jump start his love life. He looked at the plan and realized this was something a nerd might do. He never thought of himself as a nerd before; he thought he was just a socially awkward workaholic. Regardless of what he was, creating and working plans was how he had always gotten things done in the past. It was going to work for this project as well.

The plan called for frequenting places where one could meet a person of good moral character. Eric concluded that work and church were the best places to meet someone. He belonged to Notre Dames des Victoires Church on Bush Street, but it had been a while since he attended. The first step he had to take was to go back to church. Understanding that this was going to be a long-term process, Eric turned to the more immediate activity of getting dinner ready.

Mary was still getting used to the new place. She was still discovering new features like the butler's pantry and the closet in the master bath. The apartment was too big for her, and the many new strange noises were unsettling. She missed the parents that she spent most of her time avoiding. She knew that they wouldn't worry about her leaving one morning and not coming home. They knew that was the nature of their business. She had told them that she had a new assignment. They would have expected her to disappear without a word. She was sure that her parents would be fine. What concerned her more was Eric Wing.

Mary wondered if he'd remember her from the bus stop. She was nervous about her reaction to seeing him in person, so to speak. She wondered if she could disguise her emotions. She saw that she was attracted to him at the bus stop. It wasn't her fault. She had accepted the fact that they would become intimate, and now, that was all she could think about. She wondered if his body was hard and his arms strong. She wondered how his hair smelled and how experienced he was in bed. She was afraid that he would take one look at her and know that he had already made a conquest.

She made dinner and ate while reading another Chinese business book, and temporarily put her fears aside.

CHAPTER SIX

Eric was in the office at eight as usual. He took a few calls from the east coast and settled down to prepare for the meeting with the Montgomery people. He wrote down a list of everything he wanted to know about the consulting company. He was interested in their success rate and the time it took to finish a project. He suspected that there would be no end to the Montgomery Group's involvement once he started working with them. He planned to bring two people with him, Harriet Stevens and Larry Murray.

Eric had chosen Larry and Harriet to join his staff because of their strong background in the company's manufacturing processes. They had been with the company eight and twelve years, respectively. Despite their years with the company, they were still bright, alert and eager to learn new things.

Eric had told Harriet and Larry that they should come from home and meet him at the Montgomery offices at eleven. He planned for everyone to return to work after the meeting and review everything they heard and learned. He expected the review session to run late into the night. Angel poked her head in and reminded him that it was time to go. It was 10:45 AM.

Mary had slept late, but she had time enough to eat and try on two outfits before she left the apartment. She arrived at work a half hour early. She had studied her orientation package and knew the building layout. She assumed the meeting was going to be held in the tenth floor meeting room, so she went there to see how it was laid out. It was a large room that could be reduced to half its size by moving a partitioning wall. In the two room configuration, there would be room enough for a conference table and ten comfortable chairs. In this one room setup, the conference table had been removed and it was set up as a small auditorium.

Mary breathed a sigh of relief that she wouldn't be sitting around a table looking directly at the other meeting participants. She walked to Mr. Tong's office and asked his secretary where she could go to meet the other members of the team. She was escorted to an office area on the South side of the building, the side that didn't have the magnificent views of the bridge and the bay. To her surprise, there was an office with her name on it.

"The maintenance crew worked late into the night to get it ready," said Jade, Mr. Tong's secretary.

"I'm impressed."

"You should be. This isn't done for just anyone. You're getting the VIP treatment. You need to give everyone the impression that you're used to it, or else the other team members will get jealous."

Mary looked at Jade, surprised at her frankness. "I appreciate your candor," said Mary.

"You look a little shocked. Don't mind me. My position as Mr. Tong's secretary affords me a little power that I'm not afraid to use. In other words, it's not a good idea to get on my bad side."

"I understand." Mary extended her hand. "It's always

nice to make a new friend."

Jade smiled as she shook Mary's hand. "Now let's meet the other team members."

There were six people to meet, three of whom would be directly involved with the Universal Technology client. Mary was distracted and couldn't remember any of their names. She'd try to pay attention when the team was introduced to the client in twenty-two minutes. Back in her new office, Mary breathed deeply and tried to calm herself. She gathered everything she'd need for the presentation meeting. She got a note pad, a pencil, a pen and her smart phone, which she had filled with every fact she could find about China.

"It's show time," shouted Bob or Bill, one of the team members.

Everyone started to walk to the conference room. As they passed by Mr. Tong's office, Mary saw Eric Wing talking with Tong. Mary became angry with herself for being so nervous. Her anger seemed to help. She entered the room and took a seat in the back. Fortunately, all the other team members were extroverts and were jockeying for a seat closest to the chairs usually reserved for the client.

"Good morning, everyone. I'd like to introduce Mr. Eric Wing and his associates from Universal Technology Systems." Mr. Tong made the introductions as best he could. When he introduced Mary, Eric stared at her as if he recognized her. She couldn't look away quickly for fear that action would jog his memory, so she stared back and gave him a smile. He shook her hand and moved on to the next introduction.

The meeting started with a conference call with the CEO of Montgomery from the New York office. A short film was shown next, giving a history of the company and its many success stories. Bob or Bill was next on the agenda. He presented a detailed picture of everything the company offered, from connecting with key people in the target country, to entry strategies and cultural guidance. He went on for forty minutes and then had a question and answer session. He was very professional.

The potential clients had done their homework; they asked intelligent questions and forced Montgomery to defend themselves as the best choice among the available consulting companies. At the end of the meeting, Mr. Tong invited the clients to lunch at a local restaurant. On the Montgomery side, Mr. Tong, Bill and, to her surprise, Mary were to attend the lunch. Mary wasn't the only one who was surprised by the invitation. All the other team members looked at each other in disbelief. Eric thanked Mr. Tong for the invitation, but declined the lunch offer. Mary let out an audible sigh of relief that drew a sideward glance from her boss.

All things considered, the meeting went well. Business cards and informational company materials were exchanged and Eric and his people left. Almost immediately after he said goodbye to his guests, Tong called Mary into his office.

"I thought I made it clear to you that your employment here was dependent upon us getting this new client."

"You did, Sir."

"Then why wouldn't you look forward to any and every opportunity you could get to get next to the client and encourage him to come on board?" Tong was obviously upset.

"I would, but right now I have nothing to offer. Perhaps after I take some time and learn a little more ...."

"We don't have any time to waste training you. " He interrupted.

"Frankly, sir, I don't see why I was invited to go to lunch."

"Look around. In case you don't know it, you are the most attractive female on the team."

"What are you saying?"

"I'm telling you that we are in the process of trying to sign a new client. We will do whatever we have to do to get the client. If you have to sit next to a guy at lunch to get his interest, then that's what your job calls for."

"I joined the company to consult…"

"You can't consult if you don't have a client. I expect my employees to be committed and to do what has to be done to be successful. I already have people who can consult with companies to meet their goals. With you I thought I was hiring someone who could both attract a client and support his business. Was I wrong?"

"No, sir, you weren't."

"The next time you have an opportunity, I expect you to take advantage of it. You can go now."

Mary went back to her office dejected but enlightened. She now knew that the only person who didn't expect her to be a whore was her future john.

Eric and his staff went back to the office and sat around the conference table, furiously writing down everything of interest they could remember of what they had heard in the meeting. They transcribed their meeting notes into intelligible sentences. It was thirty minutes before anyone said anything. Then Larry said, "They seemed to know what they were talking about and they have a good track record working with some top companies."

Harriet chimed in, "It looks like you've got to have contacts in the target country. You have to build up those relationships over time. I came away from the meeting thinking that it's critical that we work with a consulting company whether it's Montgomery or not. It looks like it would be a waste of time trying to do something on our own. We shouldn't even make any more plans until we choose a company to work with."

"We need to meet with a few more consultants, but I like Montgomery," said Eric.

"You liked her," said Larry laughing. "You embarrassed the girl, the way you stared at her."

"She wasn't embarrassed, the way she smiled back at him. I was tempted to ask them if they wanted to be alone."

"Alright, guys, let's stay on point." Eric couldn't help himself, he had to smile. "We need to talk to those other companies as soon as possible. If we have to get on a plane to meet with them, we will. This time next week, I want to choose a company we can partner with."

"Partner with, interesting choice of words."

"Larry, you're a pain, go back to work. There's nothing wrong with choosing a company to work with and picking up a girlfriend at the same time. It's called multi-tasking."

Harriet and Larry left the office laughing heartily for the first time since they'd joined Eric's staff.

Mary was deep in thought on her bus ride to the

apartment.   She knew she could end this nightmare assignment by just failing to attract Eric Wing. She knew how to blow off guys directly or in a subtle manner.   It would be easy.   Then she tried to remember why this was such a nightmare assignment. She was living in a place she loved, and she had money and clothes. The problem was that she might have to make love to a guy she was attracted to. No, that wasn't the problem; the problem was that she would eventually have to betray a guy she was attracted to.

Seeing Eric in the meeting up close and watching him only increased her interest in him.   He was handsome, articulate and intelligent. She still couldn't understand why he was unattached. She knew herself well enough to know that she wasn't going to intentionally botch the assignment. She had to know how this story was going to play out.

She got to the apartment and changed her clothes and lay down on the bed. It occurred to her that she hadn't signed on to her personal computer in three days. It was time to check in with her handler.

For the past few days, she felt she was being handled by Mr. Tong. She wondered if Mr. Tong was more involved with her assignment than just being her employer. She turned on her computer and checked for messages.   There was nothing new. Mary sent her friend a message.

"Who can I trust at the Montgomery group?"

Mary signed off, put on her black jacket and went out. She knew where Eric lived and she walked in that direction. She didn't expect to see him on the street, but it wouldn't hurt if she did. She wanted to run into him accidently without looking like she was stalking him. She walked by his place and continued down the street.

She walked for an hour and stopped for groceries on

the way back to the apartment. After she put the groceries away, she turned on the local news and watched it while she cooked dinner. After dinner, she reread Eric's dossier, this time looking at his hobbies and interests to try and discover a way to accidentally run into him outside the work place. She had already located all the markets and grocery stores in the area, and planned to frequent them all periodically. She suspected that he took the same bus line she did, but he worked late hours and sharing a bus ride was not the atmosphere she was hoping for.

The dossier was useless for the kind of information Mary was looking for. She thought about the other members of Eric's team. If she could bump into Harriet Stevens, that might lead to another encounter with Mr. Wing. Mary checked for messages again. To her surprise, her friend had responded to her message.

"Trust no one."

"Great, that's a lot of help." Mary was pissed. "How do they expect me to do this?" Mary sent her friend another message.

"Harriet Stevens, Universal Technology employee. Provide background information asap."

She turned off the computer and took the book on Chinese culture to bed with her.

Mary woke up in a good mood, and for some reason, she was re-energized. She was anxious to get to work and get on with her assignment. She showered and dressed quickly. She read the news on her mobile phone while she ate breakfast. Before heading out, she checked her email. She had a mail message saying:

'You can pick up the news on HS anytime'.

Mary was pleased at the quick response. She had time enough to stop by the PO Box on the way to work. She wondered how the Chinese could gather the information and mail it to her PO Box so quickly. There wasn't time enough for a mail delivery. They might be able to gather information on an individual in a few hours, but it was more likely that they already had the information on Harriet Stevens. Mary suspected that she wasn't the only asset working on this assignment.

She went to the PO Box and retrieved the information on Harriet Stevens. The information was in an envelope, but it wasn't addressed and there was no postage. They had used the PO Box as a drop and someone else had a key to it. Mary's imagination started to take over. Could they be watching her? They had provided her an apartment, car and mobile phone, so it was logical to conclude that they knew where she was at all times. She thought back to everything she'd done for the past week. Had she showed any sign of disloyalty? Had she done everything that was asked of her so far? She relaxed. "Get on with it," she said softly, "get on with it."

Mary reached her office feeling a little less enthused than when she started her day. She settled in and opened the envelope retrieved from the drop box. It was basic facts about Harriet: born Harriet Johnson 8/24/63, married, mother of three, graduated at the top of her class from Santa Clara in International Relations, married Ronald Stevens, Engineering Manager at Intrix Corp, sons George and Don, daughter Carol, employed at Universal Technology for twelve years, promoted twice. There was a home address and phone number. At the bottom of the page, there was a notation that Harriet had refused two promotions that required a change of location.

Mary found Harriet's business card among the cards that were passed back and forth at the meeting. She called the number.

"Good morning, this is Harriet Stevens."

"Mrs. Stevens, good morning. This is Mary Chang of the Montgomery Group. You may not remember me; I didn't have much to say at the meeting, I just sat in the back of the room. It was my first day. I'm just following up in case there are any questions you might have."

"Of course I remember you, Miss Chang. It is Miss Chang, isn't it?"

"Yes it is."

"Of course I remember you, you made quite an impression."

"Really?"

"Yes, our Mr. Wing was really into everything you didn't say. Forgive me for being so bold, but my boss is a wonderful guy who should meet someone nice. And you appear to be nice."

"Ms. Stevens, this conversation is totally inappropriate. I'm trying to secure your company as a client. This is terribly awkward. Tell me more."

Harriet laughed and said, "I've been around Eric for years and I've never seen him react the way he did with you."

"I remember, he stared at me a little, is that what you mean?"

"Yes. For Eric, that was a big deal. Mary, I'll be frank with you, I don't know how things will work out with us becoming one of your clients, but I would like to see you and

Eric get to know one another."

"So would I." said Mary. "Could you help make it happen?"

"I'm sure I could. Just to be clear, don't agree to see Eric because you hope to nail down a new client."

"I'd love to get to know him and get a new client, but I'd like to get to know Eric, new client or not. In fact, I think the best way to proceed is to wait until after the business decision is made before project Eric starts."

"That's an excellent idea, Mary."

"Before I get my hopes up, how are you going to help us get together?"

"There are a number of ways. I could throw a party and make sure you both come unattached. I could let you know where he'll be at a certain time, and you two could accidentally meet. Just leave it to me."

"Okay, I will, Harriet. But keep in mind that it would be so much easier if we all were working together."

"I get your point. Thanks for the call; I'll be talking to you."

"Goodbye, Harriet, this may have been one of the best conversations I ever had."

Mary hung up smiling. This was great, whether or not she kept her job, she still had a shot at completing her assignment. Or maybe it was great because she had a chance of getting together with Eric. She spent the rest of the day reading company manuals on how to handle clients and memos on Chinese monetary business issues. By the end of the day she was tired. She didn't want to go back to the apartment and read herself to sleep. She thought about going to a club, but decided it wouldn't be a good idea. Eric wouldn't want a girl who was seen by herself club hopping around the city. She settled on going wild with a video and some takeout.

Eric's team had meetings with two other consultants, neither of them distinguished themselves. All of the companies had successful track records. Eric tried hard to be fair, but the Montgomery Group had the inside track. Larry was the only member of the team who resisted the choice. Eric put in a call to Charles Tong a week after their meeting to tell him the good news. Tong was delighted that he had a new client and he took his team to lunch to celebrate.

Mary was surprised at the exuberance and revelry at the luncheon. Everyone acted as if they had successfully completed the project, and not as if they'd just been asked to start one. Mary watched as everyone had a great time. After about an hour, other people from the office showed up and joined what was now a party. Mr. Tong directed Mary to a quiet corner of the restaurant.

"You still don't understand, do you?"

"Understand what?" she asked.

"In this business, it's either feast or famine. These people are celebrating the fact that they are going to remain employed for at least six more months. That's why they're letting their hair down."

"But the job hasn't even started yet. How do we know that the client will retain us for that long?"

"It will take that long before they have any idea of whether or not we're doing a good job. Have a good time, enjoy yourself." Mr. Tong turned and went back to the party.

A little after seven, Mary quietly excused herself and went home to her apartment. She had a buzz from the wine she drank at the party, but the walk from the bus stop in the cool, fresh air helped a lot. She entered the apartment and went straight to the den. She turned on her computer and checked her mail before she took off her coat. She wrote a message that the client had been obtained and then turned off her machine.

She went in the living room and flopped down on the couch, which had become her favorite place. From that spot, she could see almost everywhere else in the apartment. She hadn't admitted it to herself, but she was nervous being all alone in this enormous apartment. Surveying the place from the vantage point of the couch reassured her that she was safe there. She loved the place in the daytime, but it was a different story at night. It would be so much better if she were not alone here after dark.

It was well past dinner time. Mary wasn't hungry, but she thought she should put something in her stomach after spending the better part of the day drinking. She took a bag of salad, some cheese and cold cuts from the refrigerator and began preparing a meal, when her cell phone rang.

"Hello."

"Hi, Mary, this is Harriet. I've been trying to reach you since this afternoon."

"Sorry, we were all out celebrating."

"That was my first call, to tell you the good news. Then I thought about it and I thought I should call to tell you the bad news."

"Bad news, what bad news?"

"I wanted to tell you that project Eric is on hold."

"Why, what's wrong?"

"I realized that Eric will go out of his way to avoid the appearance of impropriety."

"What makes you think so, what did he say?"

"He didn't say anything. Trust me, I know him. I've known him for years; he will not want it to look like his interest in you influenced his decision to partner with Montgomery."

"What now, what do I do?"

"Nothing honey, just be patient. Don't expect any more stares or smiles for the first couple of weeks. Just hang in there; he'll make a move eventually. He's worth the wait."

"You know him better than I do; but remind him that I might not always be available and that he'd be smart not to wait too long."

"I'll see what I can do."

"Thank you, Harriet. I want you to know that this isn't a game to me. I really like this guy."

"Goodnight, Mary."

"Goodnight," she said, suddenly becoming aware that she did actually like the guy.

CHAPTER SEVEN

Eric and his team supplied the Montgomery team with the details of their manufacturing needs and the product family that was going to be produced in China. The information was subject to change pending the United States government review of the plans. The government had been given all the information weeks ago and still had not given its approval.

Eric and Tong arranged to meet on Friday with all the team members at the UTS office. Tong's approach to the project was that they were one team now that the contract between the companies had been signed. The team assembled in the conference room.

"Everyone, the first order of business is to plan a trip to Beijing. Everyone's passport has to be in order as soon as possible. In China, we will meet with a go-between company that will help to facilitate activities with the company that will supply component parts and assemble the finished products."

Tong took the initiative and announced his approach to starting the planned move without first discussing it with Eric. Eric ignored the courtesy breach and expressed his frustration with the government and its many requests for information that had to be formatted and submitted to conform to their standards. Tong assured him that he didn't know the meaning of frustration, but he would soon find out. He told Eric that he would be faced with a recurring theme throughout the negotiations with the Chinese. The theme being:

'Chinese workers are highly skilled and technically proficient and companies in China are interested in building products that are on the leading edge of technology. They've spent time and effort educating their workers and they are interested in work that will challenge their workers and build on their technological expertise.'

The translation is :

'We want to work with your new technology and designs so that we can steal them, clone them and sell them elsewhere.'

"All governments and companies do it. They welcome the opportunity to get their hands on the next new thing. They exploit it if they can. If they can discover a military use, all the better. If our government is afraid of giving China access, they'll drag their feet forever," said Tong.

"We can't wait forever." Eric was getting nervous.

"Of course we can't and we won't. We have to proceed as if we have full approval to manufacture the entire robotic assembly. I'm assuming that there are no real national security issues with the product."

"That's correct, there are no security issues except those in some bureaucrat's paranoid little mind."

"Okay then," said Tong. "We'll proceed as if we had full approval. That will force them to act. They'll have to either approve or explain their objection. Either way, we'll have moved the project along and completed some of the things we have to do anyway."

Eric was gaining confidence in Tong and he liked his "full speed ahead" attitude. It was obvious that Tong was taking control of the project, and Eric, although annoyed, did not object.

"If there are no problems or objections, I'll have Jade make our travel arrangements. We have a contract with the airline for special discounted flights."

"Fine, but I'd like to know more about the go-between company that we will be meeting with in China."

"We can talk about them later. First, we should have everyone schedule appointments with their physicians to get the necessary shots...."

"First, I'd like to know more about the go-between company." Eric felt it was time that he asserted himself before things got out of hand. "No one is going anywhere, unless I know why we are going and what we hope to accomplish."

Tong realized that he had overstepped, and he remembered that directing the team and leading the team were not the same thing.

"Excuse me; I let my enthusiasm get the better of me. The go-between company works with your manufacturing counter-part in China. Although it's not advertised, they also have a relationship with the government, which helps with the negotiations," said Tong. "Just like in this country, nothing important happens without government approval."

"You've met with this go-between company before, haven't you? What do we hope to accomplish by meeting with them again?"

"You and your team have to be introduced. Doing business in China is all about relationships."

"Are you saying that, if they don't like us, we can't do business?"

"No, but things will go a lot smoother if we establish a good rapport with them."

"And I suppose some money will change hands?"

"No, it won't. I will not lie to you, there is corruption and we may run into it, but with the people we work with, the exchange will be of small gifts of friendship. You need to trust me; I know what I'm doing. You may not think this trip is necessary, but it is."

"Okay, I won't ask you to justify everything that you say we have to do, but I need to see the big picture. And I need to see that we are progressing through the steps we have to take to get the job done."

"Eric, I know you're used to looking at project plans and progress flowcharts, but we first have to establish relationships. We have to gain the trust and respect of the people we're going to be working with. After we address the people issues, then we can use those management tools you're so comfortable with."

"Alright, Charles, let's get the people issues taken care of as soon as we can."

During the meeting, Eric didn't even glance in Mary's direction. Mary took it in stride with the help of a couple of reassuring smiles from Harriet. After the meeting, the two women left the conference room together and stopped in the hall.

"Just relax," said Harriet. "He'll come around in a few weeks."

"The sooner he makes a move, the better. Are you sure that our working together hasn't doomed any hope of a relationship between us?"

"Yes, I'm absolutely sure. He's just concerned about appearances. Why don't we tell Jade to seat you two together on the flight to Beijing? That ought to move things along."

"Isn't that a little too obvious?" said Mary.

"No, men are idiots. He'll think he's just lucky."

"This better work if he ever wants to get lucky."

Harriet was shocked at first, and then she laughed out loud. They looked around to see if they had attracted any attention, and walked quickly down the hall to the office area.

The trip to Beijing was a week away. It was scheduled to take five days. They were going to leave on a Monday morning and return the following Saturday. Mary was beginning to like her new life, and she was surprised to find out that she was good at her job. The other team members had more direct experience, but Mary had dealt with all kinds of people waitressing on the wharf. She could read people without exchanging a word. Just by looking, she could tell if the person was going to be warm, civil or contentious.

She was apprehensive about having to sit next to Eric for the long trip to China. She decided that she would change seats after the first leg of the trip. That would start him thinking. If he didn't make a move after being avoided, she'd take the direct approach. She'd get him alone and come on to him.

Something had to happen on this trip. Her handler wasn't impressed with Mary's friendship with Harriet. He had expected that Mary and Eric would be intimate by now. He was counting on a growing relationship and he was getting impatient. She wasn't going to be intimidated. She was trying to start a relationship that she could build on, and not just have a one night stand. Her handler would just have to be patient.

Mary had to admit that she was conflicted about Eric. Sometimes she fantasized about being with him, other times she'd think of him only as a target. She wished they could be together for real, but she realized that it could never be. If he knew the real Mary Chang, he wouldn't give her the time of day.

Charles Tong was satisfied that things were going well with the new client. Signing Universal had avoided a bloodbath at the San Francisco office. The contract was signed and he could relax for a year, until the contract came up for renewal. Tong wasn't going to take any chances this time. He was going to pay close attention to the bottom line. There were going to be no unnecessary expenses and no unnecessary personnel. He had pulled out all the stops to get the contract signed, that included hiring Mary. A little eye candy was always helpful when trying to land a new client. Now, she wasn't needed any more.

Hiring Mary had helped Tong in two ways. It served to attract and interest the client, and it also did a favor for an old friend, David Chin. David and Charles had been friends for years. David helped him get a low interest loan on his house and sponsored Charles when he joined the country club in the Eagle-Lake development. Charles didn't know what relationship David had with Mary, but since David was in his late sixties, the obvious wasn't likely.

David asked Charles to hire Mary, and he did. If the contract didn't get signed, everyone was going to lose their jobs anyway; and if the contract got signed, he could let Mary go after a few weeks. It was time to let Mary go. Charles didn't want to cause too much turmoil, so he decided to tell David that economic pressures were going to force him to let Mary go. After the China trip, he'd break the news to the team.

Charles expected the call to David to be short and uneventful.

"Hello, David, how are you?"

"Charles, I recognize your voice. I'm not usually able to tell who's calling. I'm doing pretty good for an old man."

"David, I'm sorry to say that I've called to deliver some bad news."

"What is it?"

"The young lady you asked me to hire, Mary Chang. I'm going to have to let her go."

"But why? She's qualified and capable."

"Yes that's true, but the way the economy is right now, we can't afford to keep her."

"I thought you just signed a new client."

"You are very well informed, aren't you, David?"

"I try to keep up with things."

"The fact is, we can't afford to carry her any longer, so we're going to have to let her go."

"Don't do that, Charles."

"What?"

"You did me a favor by hiring her and I did a friend a favor by asking you to hire her. You're making an arbitrary decision that will have negative repercussions. Your low interest loan hasn't been cancelled, has it?"

"No."

"The other things I've done for you over the years were appreciated, weren't they?"

"Yes, they were."

"Then don't take back the favor you did for me. That's not the act of a friend."

"What are you saying?"

"I'm saying that friends don't rescind favors. We are still friends, aren't we?"

"Yes, David, we are."

"Good, Charles, then all our prior agreements are still in place. I'm glad we had this little talk. Call again anytime."

Charles listened to the dial tone for a few seconds before he hung up. He was in shock. He wondered what was going on. *"Who is this girl?"* David had threatened him. He wasn't in control. This was wrong. He had to think back. He remembered that David had asked that she be hired, he didn't order it. He also remembered that he balled Mary out after the first meeting they had with Eric's team. He as much told her that she was a sex object for the client. Mary took it and said nothing.

It didn't make sense. *"Why is she so important? Who is David doing favors for?"* The only thing Charles knew for sure was that Mary was protected and he was vulnerable. He was angry that he didn't challenge David, but he had no real reason to get rid of Mary and David knew it. He thought about all the favors he had received, and he decided that it was best that he keep his friend for now.

Eric was looking at the calendar in his office. It had been three weeks since he got the promotion and the assignment, and in his mind, nothing had been done. He prayed that no one in upper management asked how things were going. They all had clocks ticking in their heads marking the passage of non-productive time. Sooner or later they were going to ask to see the results of his efforts. He was glad to be leaving town even if it was only for a week. The downside of the trip was that he would be expected to give the board a status report when he returned.

He packed his briefcase for the trip. He had Angel order service anniversary mementoes from the company catalogue to give away as gifts. The gifts were not expensive, just paper weights, tie clasps, pens and pointers, all with the company logo. He planned to take the weekend off and rest up for the trip. He would leave from home on Monday and take a town car to SFO.

He thought the trip wasn't an efficient use of the team's time, but he wanted to get out of the office and spending a week with Mary was something to look forward to. He was sure that there would be an opportunity for him to subtly show her that he was interested. He had already spent too much time thinking about her. It was time to find out if he had a chance to be with her or not. If she rejected him, he would be able to get back to reality and concentrate on work. If she responded favorably, he'd be happy and scared to death. Either way, he'd be better off.

He hadn't thought much about the possibility that she might actually be interested in him. If it were true, the way he felt about her, she'd have a lot of influence over him. He pictured a scenario in which she'd have him jumping through hoops, giving her preferential treatment, then the other team members would rebel and the project would collapse and his career would be over. He thought for a moment and came up with another scenario in which they fell in love, had great sex and lived happily ever after. As he left the office for the day, he thought to himself, *"It's worth the risk."*

Mary woke up in a foul mood on a beautiful Saturday morning, two days before she would go on the longest trip of her life. The trip had more significance to her than she realized. She was going to visit the country she had secretly worked for and pledged her loyalty to. It was her parents' birthplace, and she couldn't tell them that she was going. She began to be upset with everything that had ever gone wrong in her life. She recalled bad childhood incidents that she couldn't let go of. She flashed on her current situation. She was about to befriend and betray a man she wanted. She wanted to scream, but it would do no good. She felt like crying and she curled up and buried her face in the pillow.

She stayed in bed most of the morning feeling sorry for herself, then she got up and showered. She wasn't hungry and she was tired of reading books on Chinese business and culture, so she left the apartment to go for a walk. She walked in the direction of Eric's apartment building. She wanted to go to his place and move their relationship along or be shunned and go back to her life as a waitress. She wanted to do it, but she knew she wouldn't go through with it. She wouldn't do anything so stupid. She just wanted this horrible nightmare to be over.

She walked to the end of the block and was going to cross the street when someone behind her called her name. "Mary, hello."

She turned around. It was Eric, standing there smiling at her. She glared at him. "I'm surprised that you remember my name."

Eric was stunned, he had seen the look of contempt before, but he didn't expect it from Mary. "I don't understand, what do you mean?"

"What do I mean? All week in the office, you never said two words to me. It was as if I didn't even exist. Now out here in the street, we're friends?"

"I'm sorry, I didn't mean to offend you, I was just trying to establish a proper dynamic."

"How, by being friendly with everyone else and treating me like a leper?"

"No, I didn't mean to come across that way, I'm sorry."

Mary had him just where she wanted him. "Why did you single me out to ignore? Is there something wrong with me?"

"No, of course not. You're perfect. I mean you're perfectly fine. There's nothing wrong with you."

Mary smiled broadly. "I'm perfect? You were ignoring me because you like me, not because you hate me."

Eric tried to retreat, but Mary caught hold of his jacket. "Admit it, you like me don't you?"

"I don't dislike you, Ms. Chang."

Mary laughed and stepped in closer to him. "I think we're beyond Ms. Chang and Mr. Wing, don't you?"

"Alright, I'll come clean. I don't want to give the people in the office the impression that I chose Montgomery because of my attraction to you."

"Mr. Wing, the people in the office are professionals. They know that you wouldn't make such an important decision because you took a fancy to a girl in the office. And after she rejected you, they'd be sure that Montgomery was purely a business choice."

"Is she going to reject me?"

Mary looked up at him, smiled and said, "Not likely."

"I'm very glad to hear that. When I decide to make a move, it's nice to know that I might succeed."

"I'm afraid the cat is out of the bag. The move has already been made. Let's not back track. Do you have plans for dinner?"

"That's a good idea. I'm buying."

"That's a bad idea, I'm cooking."

Eric was surprised and pleased at Mary's candor. As quickly as he had formed that opinion, he wondered if it was candor or something else that Mary might be exhibiting. Maybe she was showing her experience at attracting and pursuing men. Maybe Mary wasn't the right kind of girl for him.

"If you're shocked at my boldness, don't be. I'm just tired of standing around waiting for another one of you idiot males to drum up the courage to express an interest. I've been alone for a long time because of it, and I'm tired of it. You have to get on board because it's up to you to take it from here."

Eric looked at her and asked, "What's for dinner?"

"I don't want you to think I'm showing off, so I'll cook something simple. Have you ever heard of hamburger helper?"

"Is dinner going to be a test of my affection for you?"

"It was, but maybe it would be better if we ate dinner out. I could find out what I want to know by seeing how much you're willing to spend on me, and we'd both have a better meal."

Eric laughed and they walked down the street toward the Nob Hill Café.

"Do you have a favorite restaurant in the area?" he asked.

"No, not really, but let's stay away from the touristy places. It's still early, let's just walk and talk."

"Okay."

"I'm warning you, I walk a lot. I might wear you out."

"I think I can handle it."

They walked and talked for two hours and forgot all about dinner. Neither of them realized how tired they were until they were back at Mary's apartment building. As they approached the building, Mary looked down and saw that they were holding hands. She wasn't aware of it before, but it seemed such a natural thing to be doing. She wondered if she mentioned it to Eric, if he too would be surprised.

"We forgot about dinner. Do you want to come up? We can order takeout, if you're not in the mood to be tested."

"Are you sure that's a good idea?"

Mary smiled, "Don't read anything into the invitation; I'm really an old-fashioned girl. I'm hungry and I want to know which Eric I'll be running into come Monday morning."

"Don't expect any public displays of affection, but you'll be seeing friendly Eric."

"Good, I like him much better than mean Eric."

"I think I'll say goodnight now, I have to go home and soak my feet; you did wear me out."

"Okay, enjoy the rest of your evening," Mary said,

sounding disappointed that he wasn't coming upstairs. She turned to go inside and Eric stopped her.

"You said no back tracking." He leaned in and kissed her softly. She put her arms around his waist. When the kiss was over, she held on, and they embraced.

Mary said, 'I'll see you Monday," as she went inside.

Eric was happy that everything went well and that he hadn't said or done anything stupid. He was thinking about how good she felt when they held each other. He wanted to stay with her, but he had run out of small talk midway through the walk, and he was grateful that she carried the conversation. He wondered if he stayed, would they have slept together. She said she was old-fashioned, but the kiss and embrace told him otherwise.

Mary took the elevator up to the apartment. She was partially satisfied with the way the day went. She wanted to have more time with Eric. She wasn't sure whether she'd have gone to bed with him. Her plan was to cuddle up together on the couch and watch TV. They would have ordered some takeout and seen how things went.

She entered the apartment and walked to the living room. She sat on the couch, looked around and giggled. There was no TV set in the living room. She walked around from room to room. The only set was in the master bedroom. "That would have been awkward," she mumbled. "Good thing he didn't come in with me."

She went to her computer and turned it on. She had already shared information on the upcoming trip to Beijing. She indicated that she had made one on one contact with her new love interest, and that they had spent the day together. When she was going to sign off, she got a message:

Walking around the city together hand in hand

is progress, but we'd hoped you'd be further along by now.

She was under surveillance. They had her under surveillance and they didn't care if she found out about it. She thought for a minute and she realized that she should have suspected that she was being watched. A lot of money was being spent to finance this assignment. They expected big returns from her association with Eric. She felt tired, emotionally drained. She was again bounced back and forth between the fantasy of really being with Eric and the reality of using him to steal company secrets. She had to give up the fantasy and just do her job.

She replied to the message:

I didn't know I was being watched, is there anything else I should know?

Read the attached file; follow the instructions to the letter.

Mary opened the file attachment, a word document in Chinese. The document directed her to meet with a Mr. Hui Kai at a location in Beijing on Wednesday after the evening meal. She memorized the location and deleted the file. The assignment was real to her now. If she was being watched and they had access to her apartment, she was sure that her parents were being watched and would be in danger if she didn't do what she was told. She signed off and went to bed, too tired and upset to eat.

On Sunday, Mary spent a lot of time getting ready for the trip. She checked the weather report, and packed the appropriate clothes for Beijing. When she was satisfied that she had done everything she should, she took the BMW out for a spin around the city. She drove through Golden Gate Park then over the bridge to Sausalito and back to the city. Mary drove past her parents' apartment, hoping to catch a glimpse of one of them. She knew they were all right; they were old hands at the spy game. They had probably already spotted the person watching them. They had taught her everything she needed to know, except how not to worry.

Mary went back to the apartment and put the car away. She watched the Chinese channel in bed to get used to hearing the language. She was tempted to call Eric and flirt over the phone, but she decided against it. She tried to fight romantic thoughts of him, but it was automatic. She thought about spending a week with him in the same hotel, and she suspected that their first time together would be on the other side of the world.

CHAPTER EIGHT

Eric was up early Monday morning, ready for the big trip and ready to make some meaningful progress on the China project. He was convinced that nothing had been accomplished yet. He had packed Saturday night. He was still restless after his long walk with Mary. As tired as he was, he couldn't get to sleep, so he packed. The airport limo was scheduled to come at 7:00 AM, and the plane was supposed to leave at 10:00 AM. With the security measures and traffic, Jade thought that three hours leeway should be plenty, even for an international flight.

Eric checked the apartment to make sure that everything was turned off or unplugged. He had stopped the paper and all other normal deliveries. He picked up his bags and went down to the street to wait for the limo. It was a cold, foggy morning, typical San Francisco weather. He didn't have to wait long, the limo pulled up right on time.

"Good morning, sir. Let me get your bags."

"Thank you, I'll hold on to my computer case." Eric slid into the back seat and the driver closed the door. "How many more pickups do you have to make?"

"You're my only passenger; the request was made for a private car."

"Great, I've got to remember to thank the person who made the travel arrangements."

Traffic was bad, but there were no accidents, so the cars moved slowly, but they moved. Fortunately, the driver was not a talker, and Eric was able to read the paper in peace. The trip that normally took twenty-six minutes was made in forty-five. He checked his bags at the curb and walked to the back of the security line. It took thirty minutes to get through security. Eric walked to the gate using the moving sidewalk whenever he could. He got a cup of coffee and waited for the others to show up.

He expected the ladies to be the last to arrive, but he was wrong. Harriet was the first to walk up and sit down. "Good morning, I was so excited, I stayed up all night."

"Good morning Harriet. You should have gotten your rest. You're going to be exhausted by the time this flight is over."

"I'll be alright. This is just so exciting, traveling all the way to China. I was tempted to bring my husband, but I knew you wouldn't give us any time off to look around."

"You're right about that. This trip is strictly business."

"I'm going to hold you to that."

"What do you mean?"

"I mean that it wouldn't be fair if everyone is here working and the boss decides to go sightseeing with a young lady on his arm."

"What are you talking about?"

"I'm only kidding. But I wouldn't be surprised if you and Mary plan to slip away from the group and see the sights."

"That's not going to happen!" Eric was almost shouting.

"Oh shit. Have I said something I shouldn't have?" Harriet was getting upset. "Eric, listen to me. I was just joking. I've seen the way you look at her when you think no one's watching. I think it's wonderful. You should take every opportunity you can to be with her. Don't worry about appearances; everyone knows that you two like each other. You're not hiding anything from anyone."

"Everyone knows?"

"Yes. And they also know that you are entitled to live your own life. Just remember that office hours are from nine to five, the rest of the time belongs to you. She looks like a nice girl. Go for it."

"Okay, Dr. Phil, we'll see how it goes. If I'm not fooling anyone, I'll stop trying."

"Good. I promise to keep my mouth shut and try not to interfere, but I do love matchmaking."

"Restrain yourself, Harriet; we'll be all right on our own."

Charles Tong showed up next and the conversation changed to a serious discussion of cultural dos and don'ts. Larry Murray and Mary walked up together and the conversation stopped. "Don't stop talking on account of us," said Mary. "You weren't talking about us, were you?"

Harriet said, "Eric and I were, but since Mr. Tong joined us, we were talking about work."

"What were you saying about us, Harriet?"

"We were talking about you. We were saying that you appear to balance your professional and private lives."

"I didn't know that you knew anything about my private life, Harriet."

"Yes, Eric has been filling me in."

"Hold on there. Harriet is just joking. She has a big

mouth that she can't seem to keep shut."

Harriet and Mary laughed, Eric appeared slightly embarrassed, Larry ignored them and Mr. Tong was not amused at all. Tong had been glaring at Mary since she showed up. She noticed him looking at her and she asked him if anything was wrong. He hadn't been aware that he was staring and he said that everything was fine, and that he was lost in thought. It was true; he was trying to figure out the source of Mary's power. *"Who does she know? Why is it important to have her employed at Montgomery?"* He thought she might be some higher-up's girlfriend, but the way she was throwing herself at Eric Wing disputed that theory. He couldn't figure it out.

They heard the boarding call, and lined up at the gate. Mary had gone to the ladies' room and she ended up last in the boarding line. She boarded the plane and found her seat in business class. Eric was the only one surprised that they were sitting together.

"I guess it's the luck of the draw," she said as she sat down.

"I've got to remember to twice thank the person who made the travel arrangements."

"This trip might be fun after all." Mary was getting settled and buckled her seat belt.

"This is a business trip first and foremost. Don't forget that."

"I won't. But it would be a mistake not to set aside some time for fun. It would be a serious mistake."

Eric looked in her eyes and he could see that she wasn't joking. "Okay, after the work gets done, we'll see about slipping in a little fun."

"Deal!" said Mary, as she lifted the arm-rest separating their seats.

Eric opened his paper so that she couldn't see that he was grinning. He read his paper in silence. Mary looked at the in-flight magazine and tried to relax. She didn't like to fly and having Eric next to her helped calm her. She leaned on him and he didn't seem to notice. She thought that she'd start having fun, so she pressed her leg next to his. He moved away. She was tempted to move closer to him, but she stopped. She decided to give him time to get used to having her next to him. It was a long flight, she had plenty of time. She got a pillow, leaned back and closed her eyes.

Behind the paper, Eric was keenly aware of every move Mary made. He felt her leaning against him, he felt her leg next to his and he smelled her fragrance. He couldn't concentrate on the paper; his every thought was about her. He wondered how he could have been so stupid not to accept her invitation to stay with her after their walk. Even if it only resulted in a glass of wine and a tour of her apartment, he should have stayed. He swore to himself that he would never pass up another opportunity like that one. He was going to take every step he could to get closer to her.

About two hours into the flight, Harriet came down the aisle on the way to the restroom. She stopped at their row and was going to say something when she noticed that Mary was asleep on Eric's shoulder. She smiled and continued down the aisle. Eric was enjoying having Mary sleep on him. He looked over her body. It was as if he had never looked at her before. He was able to stare at her. Her arms were slim and firm and she had a small waist. He looked down at her hips, which were wide when compared to her waist. Even asleep, her knees were together in a ladylike fashion and what he could see of her legs, he liked a lot.

He was worried that he wouldn't be able to control himself. He knew that it wouldn't be long before he'd declare his affection for her. Would she take it as a joke? She treated their relationship like a game, but she was hurt when he ignored her in the office. She seemed to be as mixed up as he was. He gently moved her hair away from her face. She moved slightly, but didn't wake up.

"Would you like something to drink?" The flight attendant and her noisy cart surprised him. He hadn't noticed their approach.

"No, I'm fine."

"Will your wife have something?"

"No, we'll let the little woman sleep for now, she'll get something later."

As the flight attendants moved on, Eric saw the corner of Mary's mouth form a smile. "Are you going to give me my shoulder back anytime soon?"

Mary's smile broadened. "I'm not sure; the little woman is very comfortable here." Mary lifted her head and straightened up. She pushed away from Eric and he held her and brought her back to him and kissed her. Mary was shocked. She looked around to be certain no one saw them.

"What was that? Why did you do that?"

"I'm tired of fighting it. I'm crazy about you and I'm tired of fighting it."

"All of a sudden, just like that?" Mary was still shocked.

"Yeah, just like that." Eric was beginning to believe that he had made a big mistake. Mary sensed that Eric didn't get the reaction that he was expecting.

"This is wonderful, but what about appearances?"

"I don't care about appearances anymore."

"Of course you do. I'm thrilled that you admitted that you care for me, but I also know that if we act inappropriately and the project suffers because of it, our relationship is dead. So let's keep up appearances and only express ourselves behind closed doors."

"Is that an invitation?"

"No," she said smiling broadly, "just a plan of action."

"Okay, I'm in."

Eric looked at her smile and he knew he hadn't made a mistake when he confessed his feelings toward her. He wanted to take her in his arms and kiss her. But he knew that she was right. He had to wait for a better time.

The trip was long and uneventful. It was Tuesday when they arrived in Beijing. They lost a day on the trip there. Everyone was in relatively good spirits. The hotel sent a car, and they drove from the airport to the city with everyone jostling in their seats to get a better look at the sights along the way. The hotel was modern and beautiful. It was built to accommodate the VIPs who attended the Olympic Games. Eric was impressed with its construction and amenities, but not pleased when he remembered who was paying the bill. The travelers were exhausted, so there were no plans made to meet for dinner, just instructions that everyone was to meet in the lobby at 8:00 AM to be taken to the meeting.

Eric's room was on the twenty-fourth floor and Mary's room was on the nineteenth. They looked at each other, indicating clearly that this was not the night they were going to be together. The long plane ride and the sixteen hour time zone difference sealed the deal; their passionate rendezvous would have to wait until they were both at their best.

Mary couldn't wait to get to her room and climb into her bed. She opened the door and sensed that something was wrong. She looked at the bed and she could make out an impression that a body might have made. She saw a note on the pillow and picked it up.

I wanted to greet you personally. I waited as long as I could. I'll see you soon.

Mary was shocked that he had been in her room. Suddenly this adventure became real to her. It hit her like a slap in the face. She was here within his reach. He could get her anytime he wanted, and apparently, anywhere he wanted. She fought the urge to panic. She picked up the house phone and rang Eric's room. "I don't feel comfortable being alone here. I'm sleeping with you tonight. I'm coming up." She hung up the phone before he could say anything.

Eric stood by the bed in his room with the phone in his hand, not knowing what to think. She didn't sound like she was coming to him as a matter of choice. He wanted nothing more than to have her with him, but something was definitely wrong. Five minutes later, there was a knock on the door. Mary was standing in the hall with her bags.

"What happened? Are you all right?" Eric reached to help her with her bags and she rushed into his arms. "What's wrong?" he asked again.

"There was a man in the hall when I went to my room. He followed me to my door. He scared me. I watched him through the peep hole until he walked away and then I called you. I don't want to go back to that room." Mary had concocted her story on the way to Eric's room. It was simple and believable, especially so, since she was shivering in his arms.

"It's okay; you don't have to go back there. We can get you another room." Eric regretted his words the moment they left his lips. "Or you can stay here with me."

Mary hadn't thought about just getting another room. She didn't mind staying with Eric, but with him, she'd have to be on her guard every second. "See if you can get me a room on this floor." He called down to the front desk and she went to the bathroom. There was a slight language problem, but he managed to get Mary a room down the hall. The bellhop was on his way up with the key.

"I hope you're not put off by my antics." said Mary as she came back into the room.

"It's okay, I'm sure I'll get used to it."

"You won't have to. Most of the time, I have my act together. Walk me to my room and I'll let you kiss me goodnight."

"I'd like my payment up front." Eric pulled her to him and they shared a kiss that Hollywood would envy.

Mary looked at him and said, "Wow, now you're going to have to help me to my room. I'm not sure I can walk there on my own."

Eric smiled. "You flatter me. Are you sure that you need to go to your room?"

"You had your chance, and you came up with an alternative."

"I've got to learn to think before I speak."

"It's better this way. If I stayed with you, you might learn too much about me. But I don't want your interest in me to wane, so I'll come to you tomorrow night. I want you to think about it all day tomorrow."

"Are you trying to drive me crazy?"

"Absolutely, I know we've been playing around, but things are about to change and I want you to take me seriously. Tomorrow will be a beginning for us.

"What's wrong with beginning today?" Eric wasn't joking. "I don't think I want to wait."

"What do you want, my body or me?"

"I'll wait; I can't handle trick questions after flying all day. I'm not happy about it, but I'll wait."

He walked her to her room. He was pissed and he planned to use his ill mood to get him through the next day until they were scheduled to be together. She opened her door and pulled him into the room. "I know you're annoyed, that wasn't my intent." She dropped her bags and started to take off her clothes. "I wanted it to be perfect our first time, but it's more important that we make love our first time and not just have sex."

"Stop, I'm all right. I can wait until tomorrow."

She stood in front of him in her slip which barely concealed her bra and panties. "Thank you. It will be worth it." She kissed him softly and said goodnight. He gave her a half smile and left. She sat down on the bed. She had pushed him almost to his limits, but she knew the easier you are, the quicker you are forgotten. She didn't want to be forgotten.

Mary took her computer out of her bag and set it up on the desk. She had had sufficient time to compose herself, helped by the distraction of the foreplay with Eric. She turned the computer on and sent a message.

You invaded my space and frightened me. Don't do it again. You've invested a lot in this venture. Don't screw it up by acting stupidly. I'm not frightened anymore, now I'm angry.

She waited a few minutes for a reply, but none came. She turned off her computer and got ready for bed. She called the front desk for a 7:00 AM wakeup call and lay down on the bed.

Suddenly, her brain turned on as if someone had flicked a switch. Why was her handler trying to contact her? They were already scheduled to meet the next day. Why did they need to meet anyway? She had no influence over Eric yet. She was doing all she could by getting close to him. What was she going to do about Eric when she got close to him? She knew that she could never hurt him. He was much more than just an objective. What was she going to do? She knew there wasn't going to be a happy ending if she continued to work this assignment. If she were replaced by another asset or got transferred or fired, she might have a way out. Her thoughts pulled her in different directions until she fell into a restless sleep.

Eric went back to his room frustrated and tired. He was aware of his feelings for this girl, but he struggled to keep things in perspective. She was beautiful and desirable, but he didn't know enough about her to emotionally commit himself to the extent that he had. He couldn't wait to be with her and make love. He thought about it and determined that there is more to love than just the physical contact. He had to find out as much as he could about her before things went too far. He was going to make that his second priority. He knew that he was kidding himself. Whoever this girl was, she was what he wanted, and not just for a night in a Beijing hotel.

Everyone met in the Lobby as planned at 8:00 AM.

They all still appeared tired. They were all looking around the lobby as if they hadn't seen it before. The furnishings and décor were beautiful. "I'll bet this place cost a pretty penny." Larry couldn't help himself. He had to make a comment. Eric mumbled under his breath. He knew he was going to be in shock when the bills started rolling in.

Harriet noticed that Mary wasn't wearing any makeup and she was dressed in a loosely fitting shirt and blouse. She was still attractive, but not nearly as attractive as she normally was.

"How are you this morning Mary? Did you sleep well?" she said so everyone else could hear her. She turned to Mary and mouthed the words: _"Did you sleep alone?"_

Mary gave her a glaring look that told her to back off and behave. Harriet returned a sheepish grin and turned to listen to Charles Tong. He announced that to save time he had secured a meeting room in the hotel to meet with their Chinese counterparts. Eric made a note to meet with Charles later and establish a budget for trips and meetings and an overall budget for the project.

They all went up to the second level to the Burgundy Room. The room was painted gray with white trim. The windows were large with burgundy drapes. There was a large conference table in the center of the room with twelve plush chairs surrounding it. Four men and a woman were in the room when the group entered. Charles Tong greeted the Chinese group and made the introductions. After a few minutes of small talk, everyone took their seats to begin the meeting. Charles began by stating that the meeting's purpose was to bring the entire working group together to facilitate their future working relationship. Everyone was to take turns introducing themselves, stating their names, background and areas of expertise.

The detailed introductions took up the entire morning. As expected, the consultants were not shy and blew their own horns. Lunch was served in the conference room to save time. The conversation around the table was pleasant and interesting. The visiting team was told about all the must see attractions in the city. After lunch, everyone was given half an hour to stretch their legs before restarting the meeting and most of the group went outside to walk the hotel grounds. Mary went up to her room to check her email for any response to her last message. Eric and Charles remained in the conference room to talk.

"It's going pretty well so far, don't you think?" Charles asked.

"It's going alright, but as far as I can see, this could have been handled with a teleconference call."

"I've been telling you all along that personal relationships here are important. You'll see that I was right as the project moves along."

"I'll take your word for it."

"I hope you do, It's also important that we trust each other," said Charles.

"Trust and respect go hand and hand in my book. And as far as I'm concerned, being wasteful with the client's money is a sign of disrespect."

"I assure you, your money is being spent wisely. I think we need to get together as soon as possible after the meeting and go over the anticipated costs for a venture this size."

"We probably should have done that before we signed the contract to work together."

"We could have, but that might have scared you off,"

Charles said jokingly.

"This isn't funny!"

"No it's not, forgive me. The truth of the matter is that the costs were going to be almost the same no matter which consultant company you chose to work with. This venture is going to be expensive. It was important for us to make a good first impression on the people we're going to be working with. And last and most important, I know what I'm doing."

"Okay, you're the expert." Eric knew he was in no position to change consulting companies. "That was a good idea, to get together and outline the expected costs, and maybe put together a budget."

Charles had expected to hold a budgeting session with Eric when they returned home to San Francisco. "Are you free this evening?"

"No, er... It would be better if I speak to the accountants to find out the details of the projected returns on the project and put the costs we come up with in proper perspective." As important as putting together a budget was, Eric wasn't going to postpone his rendezvous with Mary for anything.

"Whenever you're ready, we'll sit down and hash it out."

"Fine, I'll let you know when we can talk."

Mary entered her room cautiously. She looked around to be sure that nothing had been disturbed. She wished she could booby-trap the door to make an intruder pay for violating her space. After confirming that no one had been in the room since she left, she started her computer. There was a new message.

> *Sorry to offend you. I thought you would be anxious to meet. I am always trying to improve communications with our heroes. If you prefer arm's length dealings, I will comply.*

Mary was relieved. She wanted as little contact as possible with her handler. She was afraid he'd discover that her heart wasn't in her work. She had no idea what problems that could cause. She typed a response.

> *Meeting might compromise my assignment. An arm's length arrangement is best.*

To her surprise, she got an immediate reply:

> *You are right. The meeting scheduled for tonight is cancelled.*

Now, she was even more relieved. Yet, the abrupt cancellation of the meeting worried her. She wished she could talk to her father to get his reading of the situation. She signed off and went back to the conference room.

The team meeting continued and lasted long after normal quitting time. As the meeting went on, Mary and Eric exchanged glances and knowing expressions that were fortunately missed by Harriet. When the first day's meeting was finally over, talk started about everyone going out to dinner together. Charles suggested that they save the group dinner until the last meeting day. Eric and Mary quickly chimed in their agreement with Charles' suggestion. It was 7:00 PM and everyone went to their rooms to freshen up before dinner. A few people decided to call room service and have dinner in their room.

Mary and Eric managed to be alone in the elevator on the way up to their rooms. "Should I expect to see you later tonight as planned?" he said casually.

"Do you want to see me later tonight as planned?

"No! I want to see you now. Let's forget the planning."

Mary smiled. "I'm tired and I've been in these clothes for ten hours. I need a shower badly."

"I don't care," he said as he pulled her close to him.

"Neither do I." They kissed passionately as the elevator reached their floor. She grabbed his hand and walked him to her door.

"I thought you were coming to my room."

She giggled and said, "I think I'll let you take the 'walk of shame' tomorrow morning."

"No problem, that's a small price to pay."

She opened the door and they walked in the room. Almost immediately, she sensed that something was wrong. They heard a noise in the bathroom.

"What was that?" Mary grabbed Eric's arm and stepped close to him.

"Is anyone there?" he called out.

"Sorry to disturb you, I'm just the maintenance

technician. The maid alerted us to a plumbing problem. I knocked, but no one was here. I'm just finishing up. I'm on my way out."

Mary was frozen. She watched as the short man in overalls picked up his tool box and left. "I'm glad you were here. I don't like finding uninvited people in my room."

"It's nothing, just a guy doing his job."

"Well, he upset me. I'm shaking." She looked over at her bed and saw that someone had been laying on it, just as he had in her first room.

"Don't tell me that you are no longer in the mood."

"That's right, I'm not. I'll tell you something else. There's no way that I'm sleeping alone tonight. It will be your job to get me back in the mood. Do you think you can handle it?"

"I'll do my best." He took her in his arms.

"One more thing; let's go to your room. Suddenly, I don't mind taking the 'walk of shame' tomorrow."

"If it will help your mood, let's go."

Mary put a few things in a small bag and they left the room. Eric opened the door to his room and stepped inside first. He looked around and gestured to Mary that it was safe to enter. Mary came in and put her bag in the closet and sat down on the bed. She expected Eric to join her, but he didn't. He stood there looking at her. For the first time it hit him that they were going to make love, and not just have sex. She was beautiful and poised. He wanted to show her off. He wanted to have everyone see her with him. He wanted to know everything about her and to have her know everything about him. He wanted everything to be perfect.

"What's wrong?" she asked when she saw that he

wasn't moving.

"Nothing, I was wondering if you were hungry. Do you want to go down to the restaurant or order room service?"

"I'm not hungry right now, maybe later. You're not getting cold feet are you?"

"No, I just want things to go well. I don't want to rush you and spoil ..."

"Come here," she said. He walked over to the bed and sat down beside her.

"We're not rushing this. I don't mind if it's not perfect, but it's going to be beautiful because I care for you. If you care for me, you'll be happy with me."

He watched as she stood up and removed her clothes. She stood him up and helped him take off his shirt. Suddenly, they were both in the mood and the rest of his clothes came off quickly. He turned to switch off the light and she stopped him. "I want to see," she said as she lay down on the pillow. He heard her gasp faintly as he entered her. He tried to lower his head to her cheek, but she pushed him up and stared at his face. She had his body and his mind and she didn't want to let go of either. He looked into her eyes and watched her mouth. There were only slight indications of what she was feeling. There was a partial frown, then a quick smile followed by a grimace of pain then another smile. Suddenly, his strength left him and he lowered himself and rolled off her and exhaled as if he had been holding his breath for an hour.

"You were wrong," he said. "That was perfect. At least for me it was."

She smiled and said, "I've already admitted that I care for you, now you want me to sing your praises too?"

"Why not?"

"Alright, you were wonderful. I've never been so happy."

"Was that so hard?" They both laughed and kissed and held each other and drifted off to sleep.

When Eric woke up, it was morning. He turned to look to his left, but she wasn't there in bed with him. He came fully awake and saw her through the bathroom door. She was sitting at the vanity table applying her makeup.

"There you are," he said. "I was hoping we could continue where we left off last night."

"Sorry, it's too late for that. It's seven-thirty; you barely have time to jump in the shower, get dressed and make it down to the meeting."

"We could be late."

"One of us could be, but not both of us. I'm going to show up early just for appearances sake."

"Are you coming back here tonight?"

"Absolutely. I've taken your extra key so we don't have to come back at the same time." Mary picked up her handbag and walked to the door.

"How about a kiss before you leave?"

She went to the bed and pecked him on the lips. "I don't want to ruin my makeup," she said as she left the room. She walked down the hall to her own room and went in cautiously. She looked around to make sure she was alone, and then she turned on her computer and checked her email. There were no messages from her friend. She wrote her own message:

"I won't work with you. Inform your superiors

Robert C. Stewart

that it would be better if someone else was assigned to me. Tell them anything you'd like, but get me another contact. I won't work with you. Don't waste your time threatening me. We're done!"

She signed off and left the room. She reasoned that her handler would get into trouble if it were known that he couldn't control his asset. He would either have to change his behavior or get another assignment. Mary suspected that he wouldn't report any problems to the higher-ups.

She went down to the meeting confident that she had solved her problem or at least put it off for a while. Harriet was standing outside of the conference room.

"There's nobody in there yet. I didn't see you last night in the restaurant. Did you order room service?"

"No, I was too tired to eat, I just turned in early."

"You must have slept well; I called your room before I went down to eat. I thought you might like to join us. I let the phone ring quite a while, but I didn't get an answer."

"Yes, I slept great. I'm still getting used to the sixteen hour time difference, but I went right to sleep."

"Come clean, why don't you? You know I'm going to bug you until you tell me if you and Eric got together. I'm going to find out eventually."

"Harriet, this is not a game, this is important."

"I know I'm acting like a child, but I want this to happen. He needs someone in his life. He needs to share…"

"Relax, Harriet. He shared. And we'll be sharing every chance we get."

Harriet let out a squeal that probably alerted every

farm animal within a quarter mile that something wonderful just happened. "Oh, I'm so happy. Tell me more."

"No, this isn't high school. I don't want him to think that I ran and told everyone about us. We've still got to show each other that we can be trusted, and that we know how to keep our private business private. If I see any indication that he told anyone, he's going to have trouble. It's the same for me. Harriet, if you do anything stupid, I'll kill you."

"Okay, don't worry. I'll act like a grownup. I don't need to tell anyone, but I had to know for myself. I'm so happy for you both."

"He didn't propose. We just got together. It may turn out to be a short fling."

"I don't think so."

The team members started to show up and enter the conference room. Eric and Charles walked up together and smiled and made small talk as they went in the room. Harriet didn't see anything in Eric's demeanor that suggested that he had one of the best nights of his entire life. "He's certainly playing it cool," said Harriet, disappointed that Eric wasn't doing back flips as he walked by them.

"That's the way I'm playing it too."

They stepped in the room and took their seats as the meeting started. Neither Mary nor Harriet paid attention to anything going on in the meeting. Mary started to wonder what the next phase of her assignment would be now that she had completed phase one and had gotten close to Eric. Harriet studied Eric's face whenever he looked in Mary's direction, hoping to see signs of affection or lust. Eric was all business the entire day. It was as if he didn't have a worry in the world. He was completely focused on the task at hand. One difference did stand out. He looked happy.

CHAPTER NINE

The remaining days in Beijing went by quickly. The meetings were over and the goodbyes had been said to their Chinese partners. The task that lay ahead was to pack for the trip back home. Everyone agreed that the trip had been worthwhile, even Eric, whose opinion changed dramatically after the second day in the city. The change in Eric's opinion and his mood in general didn't escape Charles who deduced the reason for the change. Without realizing it, Charles changed his behavior towards Mary for the better. Everyone seemed to be in good spirits as they prepared for the trip home.

Eric and Mary had spent every night together except for the first one. By now everyone, including those not interested, knew that they were together and they had been together. They weren't fooling anyone, but they still were not openly affectionate towards each other. They packed and checked their tickets to verify that they were sitting together. They took a long, last look at their love nest, and went down to the lobby to join the team for the trip to the airport.

The drive to the airport was like the inbound trip. Everyone was either snapping pictures or craning their necks to see everything they could. The structures built for the Olympics were the most impressive sights. The traffic was brutal and the smog was back from its temporary break during the games. Security was tight boarding the plane, but there were no problems.

It was an morning flight, but for some reason, most of

the passengers had dozed off an hour into the flight. Mary and Eric were holding hands, looking into each other's eyes and she said, "Back to the real world. I imagine everything will change soon."

"What do you mean?"

"I mean we're not going to be roommates anymore. We are going back to having our space and slowing things down."

"That might not be a bad thing. I want to take our time and really get to know each other."

"I want to say that I know all I need to know, but you're right. We really don't know each other," said Mary.

"Not yet, but we will soon. In the meantime, I know where you live and anytime you want a roommate, you just have to whistle."

"How will I know when you want a roommate?"

Eric laughed. "You just have to check to see if I'm breathing."

They had a good flight and they talked about their childhoods and favorite experiences and memories. Mary tried to be as consistent as possible, paralleling her actual life experiences without conflicting with her cover story. She managed to paint a picture that provided some insight into the real Mary Chang. They were actually getting to know each other. And they were satisfied with what they found out.

After a few long naps and a few long conversations, they were approaching San Francisco Airport. Mary hated to fly, but she was almost sorry the flight was ending. She held his hand tightly as they came in over the water and landed roughly. They gathered their things and went to get their bags and take them through customs.

The wait to go through customs seemed longer than the flight. When they reached the first checkpoint, the line split in two and they were separated. Mary looked around and didn't see anyone from either company's team. She was led through an unmarked door and entered a room with two customs agents, a long table and four chairs. She put her bag on the table, expecting a hand search of her luggage.

"That won't be necessary, Ms. Chang. We just have a few questions," said one of the agents. The other agent said, "Our first question is, how does a waitress from the wharf land a job as a consultant with the Montgomery Group?"

Mary was stunned. She didn't know what to say, then she countered, "Don't you want to check my bag?"

"No, Ms. Chang. We're sure that an agent of the People's Republic of China wouldn't be stupid enough to try to smuggle anything into the country."

Mary collapsed into one of the chairs. Her head was spinning and it felt like all the blood suddenly drained out of her body. She was weak and she couldn't think. The agent went on. "We're not with customs, we're with the CSA. That's the Commerce Security Agency. We deal with intellectual property theft, industrial and cyber espionage, among other things.

We've been watching you for some time now. Your father taught you well. We particularly liked what you did in New Orleans."

"What are you talking about? What do you want from me?"

"Come on, Mary. Admit you've been working for the Chinese for years."

Mary finally regained her composure. She realized that they hadn't said anything specific. They were fishing. "I guess you got me. Put the cuffs on and let's get this over with." With that, she held out her wrists.

"We're not taking you in; this is just a friendly chat."

"A friendly chat in the back room of an airport and you accuse me of being a spy, but you don't want to take me in. What do you want?"

"We want you to be happy. You look like you're happy with that company executive. You two could have a good life together. Don't you think so?"

Mary remained silent. She tried to think. She assumed that if they had enough proof of the things they were alleging, they'd be taking her into custody. They were trying to scare her in order to turn her. "You don't have anything on me, do you?"

Now it was the agents' turn to be silent.

"If you could arrest me, you'd be doing it. If you're finished playing games, check my bag and let me go."

"You're right, Ms. Chang, we don't have anything on you. All we can do is bust up your little romance and mess up Universal Technology's China project."

"What do you mean?"

"When we tell the bosses at Universal that their lead executive is in bed with the Chinese government and working with spies, Mr. Eric Wing will be out of a job."

"But that's a lie; Eric is just doing his job."

"That's not how we'll spin the story. In our version, Eric will look naïve and incompetent. His bosses won't like what they hear, and Eric will be out on the street."

"What do you want from me?"

"A little cooperation would be nice. We've been watching you and we know that you don't really buy into the communist philosophy. You're an American. You've just been following in your father's footsteps even though you don't believe in his cause."

Mary was surprised that these agents really did know a few things about her. They were right about her not believing the things her parents told her when she was growing up. This country had corrupted her. She loved the western way of life. And she loved being free. The CSA Agent continued, "We want you to consider working for us. That way, you could continue working with Montgomery, taking in that hefty salary, and sleeping with an employed Universal Technology Systems Vice President."

"For as long as I live?"

"Don't worry, we'll protect you."

"I'll need some time to think about it."

"Take all the time you need. We'll call you in a few days to get your answer. Now you can go and rejoin your colleagues. Let me be the first to say, 'Welcome Home'."

Mary grabbed her bag without another word and walked back into the common terminal area. She wanted to cry, but she held back her tears and wiped her eyes anyway. They had her and she knew it was a matter of time before her little fantasy with Eric and the good life would end.

Mary didn't want to talk to anyone. She wouldn't be able to disguise her emotions. She knew that Eric would be looking for her, but she walked out of the terminal to the shuttle waiting area and was able to quickly catch a shuttle to the city.

In the terminal, the CSA agents were chuckling about the surprise interview with Mary Chang. "Did you see her expression when you said 'People's Republic of China'? She nearly fainted."

"Yeah, but she recovered quickly when she saw that we weren't going to arrest her. We should have hauled her in when she did those jobs in New York and Atlanta. We could have turned her back then."

"No, back then she was nothing, she was just running errands. Now she's hit the big time. She's sleeping with a guy who has access to leading edge technology worth millions. Now she's a target worthy of our attention. The time the agency has spent following her around the country hasn't been wasted. I knew that someday Simon Chang's kid would amount to something."

"We really haven't done anything but scared her a little and put her on her guard. We've got no real leverage to turn her. She might just cut and run."

"What, are you kidding? When we threatened her boyfriend, she almost peed in her pants. She'll do whatever she has to do to protect him. If she lets us ruin him, her assignment is blown and the Chinese will deal with her. If she agrees to work for us, she keeps him and her new life, and she will appear to be doing her job for the Chinese. We can't lose and she has no choice."

Mary rode the fourteen plus miles without saying anything other than giving the driver her address. There were three other people on the shuttle, an older gentleman and a young couple. She was on the verge of crying the whole way. Fortunately, she was dropped off first. She over-tipped the driver and went inside. Once in the apartment she ran to her bed and climbed in, crying uncontrollably.

She lay there crying and then sobbing until the phone rang. She started to answer it, but decided to let it go to the machine. "Mary, are you there? I'm still here at the airport. I got held up in customs. Those idiots didn't know what they were doing. I tried your cell, but it must still be turned off. I looked all over for you. I guess you're on your way home by now. I'll call you later. Love you."

She started crying again. She had no idea what she was going to do. She understood that she was never really in control, but now everything was way out of control. She had to think. If there was a way out, she had to find it. She undressed and got in the shower. The warm water helped soothe her and relax her. She realized that she didn't need to be relaxed; she needed to be alert and focused. She turned the nozzle to cold and forced herself to stand there until she was chilled to the bone. She dried off, put on a robe and got her laptop out of her bag. She sat down at her desk and turned on the computer. She read the message waiting for her.

I'm sorry that things did not go well between us. I am told that providing you with another contact is not an option. We have to work together and I will do my part to see that we do. As it turns out, working together will not be difficult. You have been designated to be a sleeper. There will be minimal contact between us. It may be years before you are activated. Your orders are to get as close as possible to Mr. Wing. It appears that you are on your way to succeeding.

"They want me to marry him!" Mary was shocked, but pleased that there was no need for immediate actions or decisions. A sleeper might never be activated. She and Eric could have a happy life together. In time, she might even be able to tell him the whole truth. This was good news. If she wasn't required to do anything for the Chinese, she wouldn't have to do anything for the CSA. They would have to wait until she was activated.

This was wonderful. She had gone from despair to euphoria in ten minutes. All she had to do was hold on to the man that she loved. She picked up her cell phone and held down the number "1" on the keypad. She smiled at the appropriateness of having Eric on speed dial.

"Hello, Mary, where are you?"

"I'm home. I got your message. I looked around for you at the airport, and then I hopped a shuttle and came home. We've seen enough of each other over the past week, haven't we?"

"No, we haven't. Am I going to see you tonight?"

"No, I'm beat. I'm going to sleep for a good long time. Call me tomorrow. Maybe I'll come over and cook you something."

"I'll call early and you can cook me breakfast."

"I was thinking about sleeping in and coming over later in the day to cook you dinner."

"I don't want to wait that long to see you."

"You take it easy and get your rest. Maybe it will be better if I call you. I don't want you waking me up too early. If I don't get my sleep, I guarantee that you'll be sorry. I'm going to hang up now and go to bed. I'll see you tomorrow. I love you." Mary hung up the phone, but she was too excited to go to sleep. She went back to her computer and began typing.

I received your message and I appreciate your telling me about my new designation. I will endeavor to complete my task to the best of my ability. It occurs to me that Mr. Wing would be more receptive to personal distractions if his business dealings went smoothly. I expect that we will work well together in the future.

Mary shut down her computer. She thought that the CSA might be watching her and had probably bugged her phones and were monitoring her computer. She shrugged; she wanted them to know what had just transpired. She was exhausted physically and emotionally. She doubted she could sleep, but she needed to rest to look her best before she saw Eric again.

Eric was outside the terminal waiting for the next shuttle to the city. He wondered if he should have ordered a limo. The trip had gone well and he and Mary were doing great. He felt like celebrating, but a limo was just throwing money away for a little convenience. The chilled air felt good and he was glad to be almost home. He had planned to spend the rest of the weekend with Mary. He had hoped to be going home with her and spending the night together. After the phone call it was obvious that she wanted to have some time to herself. He wondered if he was coming on too strong. The last thing he wanted to do was push her away by forcing himself on her. He decided not to worry about it and to try to give her some space.

He boarded the shuttle with three other travelers, and was treated to a trip to the Mission District, the Tenderloin and Japantown before he made it home. He had stopped the mail and the newspaper, so there wasn't anything to do but unpack and get some rest. He poured himself a glass of wine and sat in his easy chair trying to decide if he wanted to eat dinner or go straight to bed. He fell asleep before he was able to decide.

Hui Kai looked at the message Mary left for him and he laughed. He realized that she was more clever than he thought. "She wants her boyfriend's business endeavor to go smoothly. We can manage that. It's a good idea." Hui reasoned that if the business venture went well, it would eventually be expanded to include more sensitive manufactured products. Hui planned to convince his superiors to support the efforts of the Montgomery employees in China to find a company that could satisfy Universal Technology's present and future requirements. Hui also reasoned that the sooner Universal Tech was manufacturing products useful to China, the sooner he could activate his sleeper agent. The agent's sleep would turn out to be only a short nap.

Eric woke with the glass of wine on the floor by the side of the chair and with a painful stiff neck. He stretched out his arms and turned his head to look at the digital clock on the wall. He had spent his first night back home asleep in his chair. It was eleven o'clock on Sunday morning. It was a good thing that Mary was not expecting his call. He would have been late. Now, she was supposed to call, probably sometime in the early evening. He looked around; the place was a mess. It looked okay for a bachelor pad, but it wasn't neat enough to satisfy a girlfriend. He had to clean the kitchen and straighten up the rest of the apartment. He was worried about what Mary would think of a messy apartment.

Then he smiled because he thought that she might think that she was needed. He was finishing the quick clean up when the phone rang. It was Mary.

"Hello, I've been waiting all day for your call."

"That's sweet of you to say, but I know you were probably going over your notes from the Beijing meeting."

"No, seriously, I've been thinking about you."

"If you say so. The reason I called was to say that I'm still struggling with jet lag and I don't feel like doing anything. Let's take a rain check on that meal I was going to cook for you."

"That's fine, come over and we can order takeout."

"I'm trying to say that I wouldn't be very good company the way I feel right now."

"I'll make you feel better."

Mary laughed. "You're not going to take no for an answer are you?"

"You know the answer to that. I'll tell you what. I'll come over there and we'll spend some time together and when you get tired of me, you can put me out."

"You're going to bring your toothbrush, aren't you?"

"Of course not, I wouldn't think of it."

"Okay, you win. Come on over and we can talk."

"Fine, I'll see you soon." Eric hung up, grabbed his jacket, went into the bathroom and got his toothbrush and ran out of the apartment. He slowed down when he hit the street. He thought about their conversation. He remembered an article he once read that said that listening to your partner was extremely important in maintaining a relationship. She had tried every polite way she could to get out of seeing him, but he had ignored her. He wondered if he should turn around and go back home. She was expecting him now. He would spend a little time with her and leave. That way he could show her that he respected her wishes and he wasn't trying to force himself on her. That would be the plan. Be polite, cordial, but not overly affectionate, and leave after a few minutes.

Walking the few blocks to Mary's apartment did Eric a lot of good. The air was cool and fresh. The noises of the city calmed him. He decided to take a nice long walk after he left Mary's place. He pressed the button on the door panel and Mary buzzed him in. He climbed the stairs to the third floor and knocked on the door. A minute later Mary opened the door and let him in. "Welcome to my home."

She started to help him off with his jacket. He resisted. "I'm only going to stay a few minutes."

"I thought you wanted to spend some time with me."

"I do, but I don't want to force myself on you. You asked for some space and I ignored you. I'm sorry. I was just thinking about my own needs and not yours."

"And just what are your needs?"

"I need to be with you."

Mary stepped close to him and pulled him to her. She kissed him softly. "You're right, when we have the chance to be together, we should take advantage of it. We don't know how long this will last."

"What do you mean by that?"

"I mean we don't know what the future holds. We should enjoy our time together while we can."

"I understand what you're saying, but I don't like

hearing it. It sounds like what we have is temporary. I don't think of it that way."

"We ourselves are temporary. But what I'm trying to say is that even if we stay together for a hundred years, we should take advantage of every moment we have. In other words, now that you're here, I'm not letting you leave, so take your damn jacket off."

"Yes, Ma'am."

In Eric's opinion, Mary was dead wrong about not being good company. He enjoyed every minute they were together. They talked about everything and the exchange was effortless. He tried to let her carry the conversation and she did the same for him. Mary almost slipped up and revealed too much about her life. Before they realized it, it was eight o'clock at night. Mary handed him a takeout menu from the local Chinese restaurant.

"What'll it be?"

"You go ahead and order for both of us. This way I'll learn a little more about you."

"What will you learn, that I have weird tastes?"

"Go ahead, I trust you."

Mary didn't take a chance; she ordered Egg Foo Young and Shrimp Fried Rice. She didn't want him to end up with heartburn and spoil the rest of their evening. The fact that Eric hadn't come on to her or suggested getting intimate pleased her. He was looking beyond her body and showing interest in her as a living, breathing, thinking whole person. It made her want him more than ever.

"I'm sorry, I only have one television set and it's in the bedroom. Otherwise you could be watching some Pro football while we're waiting for the food to be delivered."

"It's not a problem, I'm being entertained."

"I'm happy that you're not bored. This is not like your usual Sunday, is it?"

"What do you mean?"

"I've been talking to Harriet to get some background information on my new boyfriend, and she says that you usually spend your weekends working."

"Harriet talks too much. I guess I did work a few weekends, but at that time, I didn't have anything better to do."

"So now you've got a distraction."

"I wouldn't call you a distraction, more like a more important interest."

"More important than your work?"

"Yes."

"You're kidding, we've been together for a few weeks and I'm more important than what you've been building for almost ten years. I can't believe it."

"It's true. You may not believe me now, but in time, you will."

Mary could feel her eyes filling with tears, and she quickly turned and walked to the door. "That was the bell, wasn't it?"

"I didn't hear anything."

"Maybe it was my imagination. I'm getting hungry. Back to what you were saying, I'm glad you think so much of me, but I don't want to be the cause of you not doing your job to the best of your ability."

"The job won't suffer." Eric sounded annoyed with the

turn in the conversation. Sensing his change in mood, Mary put her arms around him and said, "Don't be mad at me. What I'm trying to say is that I don't need constant maintenance. If you have to work, work. I'll be here waiting for you when you're done."

This time, the doorbell actually rang. Mary was happy for the interruption, and she sent Eric downstairs to get the food. She was concerned that things were moving too fast with him. She expected things to slow down between them once they had sex, but Eric seemed to be trying to move the relationship forward. She hadn't counted on his inexperience with women. Usually, men are satisfied with a sexual conquest. It's as if they have reached one of their goals. Then they either slow down and take a fresh look at the relationship and establish another goal, or move on to a new relationship.

He was going to push things too fast and either raise a red flag with his friends, or burn out, lose interest and break up with her. Up until now, only Harriet tried to get involved in their relationship. Mary didn't know who or what else was out there waiting for a signal to jump in and mess things up. Slow and steady was how the relationship had to go. If it went slow enough, she could be a sleeper agent for years.

They ate at the kitchen table on the everyday dishes. Suddenly, Eric looked up. "Say, it occurs to me that now that we're together, I can pick your brain about the China project. What is the next step?"

"As Charles told you, our people in China will find a company there that will be able to produce your products, according to your requirements."

"Yeah, I heard that, but Charles didn't say how long it would take to find the company."

"It probably won't be easy; a company large enough to

be a realistic candidate is not sitting around idle, waiting for us to come along. They'll look for a going concern that will have to expand to meet your needs."

"But how long do you think it will take?"

Mary thought for a minute. "It could take months."

Eric slumped in the chair and let out an audible sigh.

"It's not like a manufacturing process; deadlines and projected schedules don't apply. If everything goes well, it's going to be a long, drawn-out process. And since there are two governments involved, things will not go well. You'd better prepare yourself. This project will take a long time to get done."

"I'm sorry I asked."

"If you want me to lie to you, I will. But I'd like to confine my lying to the subject of my weight."

Eric smiled at the attempt at humor, but he was visibly upset. Mary got up and moved behind his chair and put her arms around his neck and kissed him on the cheek. "Hang in there, it'll get done."

They finished dinner and did the dishes. It was a little after ten and Mary got Eric's jacket and handed it to him. "I see you decided to kick me out after all."

"It's late, and I'm tired, so you should brush your teeth before coming to bed."

Eric went into his jacket pocket and got his toothbrush. "You're on top of this relationship, aren't you?"

"Most of the time. You can be on top when it counts."

CHAPTER TEN

Back in the office on Monday morning, everyone was curious about the trip to Beijing. Eric had to field questions about the trip the moment he hit the door. He was sorry that he hadn't done more touristy things so he could sound more interesting to his co-workers. He had been smart enough to remember to bring back some cheap souvenirs for a few of his associates and a pair of gold earrings in a silk purse for Angel.

The most important item on his agenda was to secure the government's agreement that the entire robot assembly could be manufactured in China. If there were restrictions or limits placed on what could be manufactured, he had to know about it as soon as possible. If there were restrictions, the team in China would have to modify their search for a manufacturer.

While Eric was in Beijing, Bob Watson had been negotiating with Washington, but he had gotten nowhere. Bob said he had been passed around by the bureaucrats in Homeland Security for most of the week. He had several phone numbers that he happily gave Eric, signaling his withdrawal from the negotiations.

Eric looked over the list of numbers with associated names and titles, none of which looked relevant to what he wanted. He called the last name on the list, Richard Spicer, Deputy Under Secretary – Domestic Product Review.

"This is Rich Spicer, how can I help you?"

"Good Morning, Mr. Spicer. My name is Eric Wing.

I'm with Universal Technology Systems. We've been seeking approval to manufacture one of our product lines offshore. I have a case number here if you want it."

"That's not necessary, Mr. Wing. I received word late last week that Universal Technology's request has been approved to manufacture the complete product assembly in China."

"That's wonderful. When will we be receiving the written authorization?"

"You can expect to receive the signed authorization in two weeks."

"Great, is there anything else we need to do on this end?"

"Not really, we'll be contacting your legal department to tie up some odds and ends."

"Thanks, Mr. Spicer, that's all I need to know. You have a good day. You've already made mine."

"Goodbye, Mr. Wing." Spicer hung up the phone and looked across his desk at the two CSA agents sitting in his guest chairs.

"Are you sure this is what you want to do? Aren't we giving the Chinese access to advanced military grade technology?"

"No, we've been replacing the chips in the robot assembly for months. We have a subcontractor modifying all the Universal robots shipped to the government. The Universal chips are no longer compatible with our military guidance systems. By the time the units are manufactured in China, they'll have no military value at all."

Spicer sat back in his chair and tilted his head. "But what are you accomplishing by going ahead with the technology transfer?"

"We're identifying the Chinese agents on American soil, we're providing a red herring for the Chinese and the product is still good for non-military purposes, so Universal will be able to make a buck or two. Everybody's happy."

"Is there anything more I can do for you gentlemen?"

"No, we'll take it from here. Thanks for your help." The two agents got up and left Spicer's office. They walked down the hall to the elevator. As they got in the elevator, one of the agents said, "Now we've started the ball rolling. Our little Mary can start to be of benefit to the Chinese by trying to influence the boyfriend or by getting access to sensitive information."

It had been four days and Mary was still feeling sorry about how the conversation with Eric about work had gone. She wanted to get him to agree to never talk about work again, but she knew that would be stupid. Sooner or later, she would be forced to chat Eric up about work and his plans for Universal and China. She had not seen him in four days and she didn't have plans to see him today either. She missed him, but she was relieved that she had some time to rest.

She was still waiting to hear from the CSA. She thought it might not be the worst thing if she refused to cooperate with them and they exposed her. Then she'd be out of it. Maybe they wouldn't make good on their promise to ruin Eric. Maybe they would. She couldn't take the chance. She'd have to go along with them. Whatever she did, she could see it ending badly. She planned to try to concentrate on work and not call the CSA. She also hoped that they wouldn't call her.

Five days after they ambushed her in the customs' office, the dreaded call came.

"Hello, this is Mary Chang."

"Good morning Ms. Chang, this is Agent Morris of the CSA. I realized after our meeting last week that we were never properly introduced."

"You were so busy attempting to blackmail me that you forgot to use proper etiquette."

"I guess that's true, I did have a point I wanted to make. Now that you've had some time to think about it, have you decided to accept our proposition?"

"I'd like a little more time to think it over."

"I'm sorry, Ms. Chang, but your time has run out."

"I don't really have a choice, do I, Agent Morris?"

"No, you don't."

"Okay then, I'll do what you ask. Since you're probably taping this conversation, I want to make it clear that I have done nothing wrong. I'm doing this because you've threatened to lie to Eric's bosses and ruin him."

"No one's taping anything. We need to meet in person, and I'll give you your orders. Stop in your local grocery store on your way home tonight. You'll be contacted. Have a nice day."

Morris hung up the phone and turned off the recorder. "Smart girl, now that recording is useless, unless we want to incriminate ourselves."

Morris' partner, Agent Ben Coleman, shrugged. "She actually loves the guy or else she would have told us to get lost."

"Yeah, that's the only chip we've got, so we'd better not push her too hard."

"I don't know. If she's really hooked on the guy, we might be able to get her to do anything we want."

"You never can tell with spies, it could all be an act with her."

The phone went dead and Mary knew she was trapped. All she could do was go along. She relaxed a little when she realized that nothing was going to happen anytime soon; after all, she was a sleeper. Mary thought for a moment and remembered that her handler had written to her about her and Eric walking together hand in hand. She was being watched in her neighborhood and couldn't meet with the CSA in the local grocery store. She had to cancel the meeting, but she didn't have a way to contact agent Morris. She decided to risk not showing up for the meeting. She weighed the possibilities and determined that it would be better to be branded unreliable than to be killed.

Mary was suddenly calm. She wasn't worried about her predicament. It was as if she was resigned to the fact that it was just a matter of time before her world would come crashing down around her, and she didn't care. She never intended to hurt Eric, so she told herself that she had no reason to feel guilty if he got hurt. What she was doing for the Chinese was about company secrets, not government secrets, so she was not a traitor. She was just a pawn, a tool. You can't blame a tool; it's the workman who's at fault. "I did nothing wrong, I did nothing wrong..."

The phone rang and startled her. It was Eric.

"Hi, Sweetie, how's your day going?"

"Good afternoon, Mr. Wing, everything's fine. How are you today?"

"Is someone there with you?"

"No, I'm alone."

"Are you mad at me, have I done something wrong?"

"No, I'm not mad, but I think that business hours are for conducting business. And I don't think it's a good idea to start calling each other familiar names like 'Sweetie' or 'Honey' or 'Babe', etc. I've worked hard enough to earn some respect for the job I do, and if someone overheard you referring to me in that manner, all my hard work would have been for nothing."

"I'm sorry, I'm sorry. I won't do it again. Is that all that's bothering you?"

"No, there's something else, but it can wait until later. Call me tonight at home. Now, unless this is a business call, I have to get back to work. Goodbye."

Mary hung up with mixed feelings about the call. The idea of forcing Eric to dump her came to her the moment she heard his voice. She didn't want to lose him but it would be better for both of them. Without the threat of ruining Eric, the CSA had nothing on her. And if Eric no longer wanted her, she could be returned her to her former life. It was the perfect way out. The only casualty would be her love affair with Eric.

When Eric hung up the phone, he felt that he had just stepped off a cliff. He couldn't understand what went wrong. He tried to remember their last conversation. He remembered that everything was fine. He left her place Monday morning after having a wonderful Sunday night. He hadn't called her in two days, but she was always the one wanting more space. He was tempted to ask for help from Harriet, but decided against it for now. He'd wait and call her tonight, as she asked. He thought to himself that it might be a women's thing. It was going to be a long day.

Mary shuffled papers and answered phone calls, but she didn't do anything constructive all day long. She couldn't get Eric off her mind. She didn't want to be cruel, but if he didn't catch on, she'd do what she had to. The day dragged on and on until mercifully, it was five o'clock. She locked her desk and packed her things and left.

She was a little worried that agent Morris might do something stupid, but he was supposed to be a professional. He wouldn't make good on his threats too quickly and blow his chance at getting what he really wanted, a double agent. The bus ride home seemed like it took forever. She got off the bus and started walking. She quickened her pace and took a deep breath when she reached her building. She entered the apartment and sat on the couch, motionless for ten minutes while she reviewed her plan and its possible consequences. She confirmed that breaking up with Eric was the best course of action. It had to be done carefully. She couldn't go from a loving, sweet girlfriend to a venom spewing psycho in one easy step. The transformation was going to take time. Her cell phone rang and she fished it out of her purse before the call went to voicemail.

"Where the Hell are you?"

"Hello, agent Morris, how nice to hear from you again."

"Cut the crap, why didn't you show up as planned?"

"Why didn't I show up as you planned? I'll tell you. I'm under surveillance in my neighborhood, and it's a good idea not to be seen talking with the CSA around here."

"Why didn't you tell me that you were being

watched?"

"First of all, you didn't give me a chance and second, I don't have any arrangement with you yet, so it's none of your business."

"If you know what's good for you, you'll…"

"Hold that thought, Agent Morris, I have another call."

Mary pressed a button on the phone. "Hello, Eric, hold on. I have to clear my other call."

"Agent Morris, I'll have to call you back. If you give me your number, I'll get back to you as soon as I can."

Morris gave her the number and said, "You're playing a dangerous game, Ms. Chang. Be careful."

Mary switched calls. "Eric, I'm sorry I snapped at you earlier, but I've been thinking about us and I think we've gone too far too fast."

"Mary, if I've done anything to upset you, I'm sorry."

"You haven't done anything wrong, you were just being you. You acted like any man would."

"Are you saying that I took advantage of you?"

"No, not exactly, but I did feel intimidated by you in Beijing. I wasn't sure what would happen if I refused your advances."

"Mary, be serious, you were more aggressive than I was."

"I'm sure you see it that way, but now I think we should slow down."

"Maybe we should back up."

"I expected you to say something like that now that you got what you wanted."

"You wanted it as much as I did."

"I don't want to argue with you, all I am asking is that we slow down and take a look at what we're doing and where we are going."

"Fine, let's do that."

"Good, then we're agreed. I have to go now, that was my Ex on the line, I have to get back to him. I'll see you soon. Bye."

Mary hung up with a sick feeling in the pit of her stomach. It had to be done. She didn't think she had said enough for Eric to dump her, but he would surely take a good hard look at the girl he thought he was falling for. She felt stupid for letting herself get so involved. The relationship was based on a lie; it had to end in disaster. She started to weep.

Eric was stunned. He sat there in his office staring at the phone. He couldn't figure out what went wrong. They were genuinely happy and in love up until today. He had never heard her mention an Ex. In fact, she didn't say anything about her past relationships. She didn't talk about them and he didn't want to hear about them. As beautiful as she was, she must have had other men in her life. Maybe one of them was giving her trouble. If she wanted his help, would she have asked for it? He didn't know.

"I'll let a few days pass and then I'll talk to her face to face."

Eric tried to get back to work. He had been in good spirits before the call to Mary. Charles had called him and told him that the Beijing team had found a company that met all of Universal's requirements. The company, Chuan Chen Ltd., had an excellent reputation and they were willing and able to expand if necessary. Eric had been excited that the project was finally moving forward. Charles had also assured him that there would be minimal Chinese Government involvement.   Eric was going to tell Mary the good news, but after she said her piece, he forgot all about the China project.

He spent a few minutes trying to get back to work and couldn't. He tried to concentrate, but his mind kept drifting back to her. He had to talk to her now, face to face. He picked up the phone and dialed her number.

"Haven't we said enough to each other today?"

"Mary, we need to talk in person."

"That's not necessary and I don't want to see you."

"I'm coming over, and I'll pound on your door until you let me in."

"No, don't..." Mary heard the line go dead. She was afraid that she couldn't continue with the charade if Eric was looking at her. She thought that she would weaken if she saw hurt in his eyes. She had to be strong; this was for his own good. She paced and rehearsed the things she planned to say to him. Nothing sounded convincing. She thought about running, but she knew that she had to face him eventually.

She went to the kitchen and made some tea to calm herself down. On the way back to the living room, she passed a wall mirror and saw her reflection. Her eyes were puffy and red. She ran to the bathroom to wash her face and try to look presentable. Eye drops and a cold wet towel helped some, but she didn't look well.

The knock on the door startled her. It seemed like only minutes since he had called her. She didn't want a scene with her neighbors in attendance. She opened the door and stepped back to let him in. "I don't want any trouble, Eric."

"Neither do I, but I do want an explanation."

"I've already told you; we're moving too fast."

"We weren't moving too fast four days ago. What's changed since then?"

"Don't I have the right to express how I feel whether or not it's what you want to hear?"

"This doesn't make sense, you said you loved me. Have you changed your mind about that?"

"Yes, can't you accept that?"

"No. I can't and I won't."

Mary made her way to the couch and sat down. "Damn you, Eric, just let go."

Eric sat down beside her and reached for her hand. She pulled her hand away and said, "Don't touch me."

"I need to understand, and I'm not leaving here until I do."

Mary looked at him with an expression of frustration mixed with anger. "You want to understand? Okay, here's what you need to know. Our getting together was no accident. I was directed to get close to you and I did."

"By whom?"

"You don't need to know that. What you do need to know is that our little affair has gone on long enough."

"But why would you do this? What has it accomplished?"

"You hired the Montgomery Group didn't you? Now it's too late to change firms, so there is no need to continue our romance. I will admit, it was fun, but it's over now. I tried to let you down easy, but you wouldn't have it."

Mary could see Eric disintegrate before her eyes and she hoped she could get rid of him before she broke down.

"I think you'd better go now. If you want to discuss it further at a later time, just let me know." Eric left as quickly as he could. He wanted to get away before he did something crazy. His head was pounding like a jackhammer and his eyes were full of tears. He had never felt such pain. He paused at the top of the stairs and tried to steady himself. He still didn't believe it. He tried to think. Could she be telling the truth? No, he remembered settling on the Montgomery Group before he was serious about her. She was lying. Why?

He turned and walked back to her door. He lifted his hand to knock and he heard her inside crying loudly. He lowered his hand and listened for a moment. She was in as much pain as he was. She had created the situation and now she was suffering because of it. He turned and went down the stairs and outside. His mind was racing as he walked. She wanted this. It hurt them both, but she still wanted it. He was still convinced that she loved him. He decided that he had done enough for now. He'd wait and see what happened. He'd leave her alone and just wait.

CHAPTER ELEVEN

Mary cried most of the night. She couldn't sleep or eat. She knew she had hurt him badly. She also knew that she had to get over it. She didn't expect to have to see Eric at work and now they wouldn't be seeing each other outside work. Now the CSA had nothing on her and since she and Eric were no longer together, they couldn't tell Universal's upper management lies about Eric working against the company's best interests. The only fallout was that she had failed in her assignment to stay close to Eric.

After a terrible, guilt-filled night, Mary was getting ready for work when the phone rang. "Hello."

"Hello, Hell! You never called me back."

"Good morning, Agent Morris. How are you this morning?"

"I told you what would happen if you didn't cooperate with us. Didn't I?"

"Yes you did."

"Well, what's it going to be?"

"Agent Morris, I've decided not to have anything to do with you."

"You asked for it. When I'm done, Eric Wing will be out on the street without a pot to piss in."

"Go ahead, do your worst, I could care less. The bastard dumped me."

"He did what?"

"You heard me. I wish you would screw up his career. It would serve him right. I have to get to work now. You have a nice day." Mary hung up and left for work.

Morris slammed down the receiver. "Shit! She said that Wing dumped her and she doesn't care if we burn him."

Morris' partner, Ben Coleman, countered, "Maybe she's bluffing."

"It's a risky bluff. If she hasn't lost him already, she will if we burn him and out her. I don't know what she's up to, but we'll watch her closely and see if she's telling the truth."

"Yeah, they looked like they were really hot for each other. If she's lying, they won't be able to stay away from each other for long."

Mary went to work thinking that she had all her major problems solved. She knew her emotional problems had to be ignored for as long as possible. She tried hard to focus on work and made no attempt to contact Eric. The work days passed by quickly, but the nights at home were long and lonely. She knew she was being watched by the CSA and they probably had her phones tapped. She forgot about the other neighborhood surveillance.

One evening about a week after her confrontation with Eric, she got an email.

It's been reported that you have not been seen with Mr. Wing for several days. Are you having any problems with your assignment?

Mary stared at the screen for several minutes. She tried to think of the best way to respond. She was trapped. If she got back together with Eric, the CSA would squeeze her; if she didn't get back with him, her handler would give her trouble. She wanted to run. Then it came to her.

I've been blown. The CSA is on to me. I had to break up with Eric to try to cover my tracks. I didn't contact you earlier because I thought I was being monitored. They want to turn me. What should I do now?

She looked over her response and smiled. This was the way out. They had to abort the assignment now. She signed off, went to bed and slept well for the first time in over a week.

Eric had buried himself in his work. The project was moving along well. Charles had suggested taking another trip to China to meet with the management of Chuan Chen Ltd and to start looking for housing. According to Charles' plan, Eric and his team should move to Beijing and plan to live there for about two years before being rotated out. Eric hadn't been enthused about the plan, but since the flare up with Mary, he was warming to the idea of spending two years out of the country.

Once the team moved to China, there would be no need for the support staff. Eric had been working to place Angel and the other two secretaries who worked for his team. He was going to find a suitable spot for Angel even if he had to go outside of the company. He was secretly glad to have an important distraction, otherwise Mary would have filled his thoughts, and he would have been acting like a sulking schoolboy.

To his surprise, each day without Mary was a little easier than the last. He was pissed at her, but he didn't believe her tale that she was only interested in him to secure the Universal account for the Montgomery Group. He sat back and put his hand on his chin for a minute, and then he picked up the phone.

"Good morning, this is Charles Tong. How can I help you?"

"Charles, this is Eric. I've heard something disturbing from one of my colleagues. He said that your company has been known to provide young women to potential clients in order to secure their business."

"That's outrageous!"

"That was my first thought. Then I remembered being befriended by your Mary Chang."

"The accusation is not true, and as for our Mary Chang, if you saw her resume, you'd know that her talents lay in the area of international business. It is also my understanding that a relationship developed between you and Ms. Chang after you became a client with us."

"Quite right, Charles, but I had to bring the issue to your attention. A rumor like this could reflect badly on us with my board. I'll do what I can to see that it goes no further."

"Good. Lies like that aren't welcome. Eric, while I have you, have you set a date for your next trip to China?"

"Not yet, but I'll let you know the date before the end

of the week. By the way, how many members of your team are expected to make the trip?"

"Just me."

"Good, that will cut down the expenses. Okay, that's all I have. You have a good day."

Eric was more convinced than ever that Mary lied. He also got the feeling that she was trying to protect him. He knew that he would eventually break down and call her, but he thought that she needed a little more time.

Mary woke up late and checked her email for a reply. There were no messages for her. She went through her morning ritual of washing, getting dressed and putting on her make up, then eating a breakfast of tea and toast. She checked her email every ten minutes until she left the apartment. Still nothing. She looked intently at every passerby on the way to the bus stop. She studied all the faces on the bus. She felt that she was being watched and everyone looked suspicious. At work, she turned on her computer and waited.

The time passed slowly until just before 11:00 AM. She got her reply.

Cooperate with them.

She couldn't believe it. She was completely confused. In order to cooperate, she would have to admit that she was working with the Chinese. She would also have to reconcile with Eric. Her relationship with Eric was key to the interests of both the Chinese and the Americans. She thought for a moment and she began to type.

That was an insufficient response. Should I tell them the truth? How much information should I divulge? Has my primary objective changed? I need more details.

Mary stared at the screen waiting for the next message, but nothing came. She tried to understand the thinking behind the idea of cooperating with the CSA. Were they planning to give the CSA false information? She couldn't make sense of it. The only thing that came through loud and clear was that Mary Chang was still in deep trouble.

Suddenly, everything started to clear up and she realized that there was nothing she could tell the CSA that they didn't already know. They knew she was working for the Chinese. They knew she was supposed to get close to Eric to influence him. They knew who her parents were and what she did before she worked for the Montgomery group. They knew it, but they couldn't prove any wrongdoing.

She decided to do nothing. She would wait to see if Eric would call. If he did, she'd make up with him. If agent Morris called again, she'd work out an arrangement with them to protect herself, and then she'd tell them whatever they wanted to know. The thought of being close to Eric again made her smile. The smile didn't last long when she remembered that the CSA would use her relationship with Eric as a club to get her to do whatever they wanted. She couldn't worry about that now; she'd tell Eric everything when the time was right.

Time was moving slowly for Eric as well, he was counting the hours until he'd call Mary again. He thought one more day would do it. Either he'd get her to agree to meet and have a rational conversation, or it would be over between them. He wasn't sure that he could give her that ultimatum, but he had to try. He tried to busy himself with work, but he kept looking at his watch, counting the hours until he'd make the call.

He had scheduled a team meeting in the afternoon to review the status of the project. This reminded him that Harriet and Mary seemed to be close during the China trip. Mary never mentioned being friends with Harriet, but he remembered seeing them together in the airport and outside the meeting room in the Beijing hotel. Eric didn't want to involve Harriet in his personal business, but if she had some insight into Mary's behavior, maybe she could help. Eric called her.

"Universal Technology Systems, this is Harriet."

"Harriet, this is Eric."

"Good morning, Boss. What's up?"

"I wanted to talk to you about Mary."

"I'll be right in." The line went dead before he could stop her from coming to his office. She was there before he could hang up the phone.

"Is everything alright? I haven't spoken to Mary since the China trip. She seemed very happy and I got the impression that things were great between you two. Did you do something stupid?"

"Slow down and catch your breath. I just wanted to know if she confided in you. I was wondering if she said anything to you about us."

"Is there a problem?"

"Yes. Out of nowhere, she put the brakes on. She said things were moving too fast and we needed to slow down. Then she said that she was with me just so Montgomery would get our business. She's trying to dump me, but I don't know why."

"I'm sorry, Eric. Mary and I aren't close. We just shared a little girl talk on the trip. I can tell you that she was serious about you. I'm sure of it. You need to talk to her."

"Okay, I'll try again."

"Sorry I couldn't help. Don't give up on her."

Harriet left the office looking heartbroken. Eric was sorry that he had talked to her, now another person was miserable. Harriet did confirm that his planned course of action was the right one. He had to call Mary and talk it out. He'd wait and call her in the morning.

Mary was confident that she hadn't completely destroyed her relationship with Eric and she wasn't worried about patching things up with him. She was worried that she would again be vulnerable to the CSA. She was also worried about her handler. Of what value could she be to him if she was cooperating with the CSA? Things were getting crazy.

Mary decided to warn her parents to be ready to run. She would stay at work late enough to make a short call from a coworker's phone to an answering service, and she'd leave a message for Dr. Lester. Within minutes her parents would be alerted. It was an early warning system her father had worked out with her years before. They would receive another message a day later that everything was all right, or else they were supposed to quietly disappear.

Mary dialed the number Agent Morris had given her.

"Morris."

"Agent Morris, this is Mary Chang. How are you?"

"I'm just fine, Ms. Chang. What can I do for you?"

"I wanted to talk to you about your offer."

"What offer?"

"When we first met, you asked me to consider working for you. If the offer is no longer on the table, I'll say goodbye. I'm sorry I bothered you."

"Wait! Don't hang up. The offer is still on the table. What made you change your mind?"

"The truth is that you were right about me. I do love this country. I have not done and would not do anything to hurt it."

"Right. What can you tell us about your organization and your role..."

"Let's slow down. "I'll agree to work with you and tell you everything I know, but first I'll need a signed agreement that I will not be charged with any crimes against the U.S. Government."

"I can't agree to that."

"You'll have to. Otherwise, we have nothing to talk about."

"I'll never be able to get an agreement like that signed for a foreign agent. Who knows what you've done?"

"I thought you knew exactly what I've done. At least, that's what you told me. Look, agent Morris, you have nothing on me now. In order to work with you, I'll have to incriminate myself. Do you honestly expect me to do that without protection from prosecution? If you want my cooperation, give me what I want."

"I don't ..."

"Take it or leave it." Mary hung up the phone. She knew that the CSA had no choice if they wanted her cooperation. She cleaned off her desk and went into an office down the hall. She made a quick phone call and left for the evening. Mary felt relieved after the call. It comforted her to know that her parents would be on their guard.

Mary believed she was in good shape with the CSA and Eric, but Beijing had her worried. She wondered what they had in mind for her. This operation wasn't that important, and it might take years before Universal made anything technologically significant in China. Even then, it would be under close government scrutiny.

She was deep in thought and nearly missed her bus stop. She went in the apartment and straight to her computer. She didn't find any messages. She walked around the apartment trying to think. One thing she could do was to put her love life back in order. She fished her cell phone out of her purse, and then she put it back. She thought about going over to Eric's apartment, and then she remembered that he often worked late. She got her phone and called him at home, planning to leave him a message. He picked up.

"Hello."

"Hello, Eric, we need to talk."

"I thought you wanted me to leave you alone."

"Do you want to talk to me or not?"

"Yes, of course I do. Do you want me to come over?"

"Yes, I do. I could come over there if you want."

"No, it's too late for you to be out by yourself. I'll be right over."

Mary smiled as she ended the call. "He thinks it's too late for me to be out. He's still sweet to me in spite of what I've put him through." She made up her mind that she would never hurt him again. She ran to the bathroom to freshen up.

After a few minutes had passed, there was a knock on the door. She opened the door and let him in. She couldn't read his expression. He looked annoyed and hurt and happy to see her all at the same time. She didn't say anything; she just walked to him and held on. He wrapped his arms around her and held her tight. They didn't speak for a long time. Eric slowly released his grip, but she didn't let go. Instead she started to cry. "I don't know what to say. I was scared; I am scared."

"What's there to be scared of? I would never hurt you."

"It would hurt if you'd leave me, and I didn't want to wait until it happened, so I decided to leave you."

"I don't understand."

"Okay, I'll explain it to you. Part of what I told you was true. I was told to meet you and to get close to you."

"Why and by whom?"

"Because you are a senior executive in a major technological company, I was asked to become your lover by the People's Republic of China."

Eric was stunned. "Bullshit! You can't be serious."

"It's true, I've worked for them for years and so did my parents. We did not perform any treasonous acts, although my parents would have if asked. Industrial espionage is what we were doing. Before this, I delivered messages, picked up and delivered packages and information."

"So this was all a job for you?"

"Hear me out please. I didn't have to confess this to you. I'm telling you the truth because I love you."

"I'm listening. Is there anything else?"

"Yes, I'm not an expert in international business. I have a degree, but I was waitressing before I got the job at the Montgomery Group."

"How did you get that job?"

"I was provided a new background and resume and I guess somebody put in a good word for me."

"What did you expect to get from me?"

"I don't know what they wanted. I suspect they were after company secrets."

"Now you're coming clean because you couldn't keep up the charade. Is that it?"

"No! I could have played my part until our grandchildren had children. I'm coming clean because I got caught. The CSA is on to me."

"The CSA, I can't believe this. You're telling me that you are about to be arrested by the CSA?"

"No, they're on to me, but they haven't got anything on me. I could walk away now with no problem. The CSA would probably watch me for the rest of my life and my friends in Beijing would disavow me, but I'd be home free."

"Is that all?"

"No, there's more. The CSA wants me to work with them against Beijing. If I don't work with them, they threatened to tell your bosses that you are consorting with a spy and should be replaced."

"But I haven't done anything wrong."

"It doesn't matter, it looks bad for you. It was poor judgment on your part, getting involved with someone like me. And the CSA promised to embellish their story to get the result they are looking for. It boils down to this, if we're a couple, the CSA has the leverage to make me work for them; if we are not a couple, we can go back to our old lives, no harm done."

"It sounds like a no-brainer. Why didn't you just stay away?"

"You kept trying to understand what was wrong. And you kept trying to get me back. I thought if I told you the truth, you'd know where we really stood."

"Mission accomplished."

Mary folded her arms across her chest. "The CSA is probably watching the place right now. I love you, but I want you to think about this. The decision has to be yours."

"There's nothing to decide. I've got to go."

Eric walked to the door without looking at her and left. As he exited the apartment building, he was spotted by agents Morris and Coleman, sitting in their car parked across the street. They watched Eric pause at the corner and walk up the hill toward his place.

"I guess he's not spending the night tonight."

"She might have been telling the truth about the breakup."

"We should have had her place bugged, then we'd really know what was going on."

"It looks like we'll have to find another angle to use to

get her cooperation."

"Well at least we can sleep in our own beds tonight."

Eric walked past his apartment building. It was cold and he had on a light jacket, but he didn't feel a thing. He was numb inside and out. He had been betrayed from the start. She lied and she was never really interested in him at all. It was all a game to her, a job. She was a spy from a family of spies. She had used him and she was still trying to use him. He kept walking and thinking.

He tried to remember every one of their conversations. Had she given him indications that something was wrong and that she wasn't really invested in their relationship? He couldn't remember anything that she said or did to give herself away. His numbness was replaced by anger. He kept walking. The anger boiled up inside him with every step. He had loved her and she betrayed him.

He was her long range plan, her path to company secrets. She had been caught by the CSA and she still wasn't giving up on her plan. She was still trying to use him. He thought it was a smart move on her part to confess to him. If he forgave her, she could still complete her mission.

His head was filled with thoughts of anger and pain and love and hate. He reached the end of California Street and turned around. He began to feel the cold, but he still needed to walk and think. He had to control the pain and anger. He needed to dismiss any thoughts of love. He had to get free of her.

On the way home, he began to think more clearly. He remembered making love to her in Beijing and their conversations on the long flight home. She did feel something for him. It might have been love. But that was weeks ago. Now there was no love and no trust. It was over. By the time he made it home, he was exhausted. He flopped down on the bed and fell asleep.

Agents Morris and Coleman had driven by Eric and realized that he had passed his building. Just out of curiosity, they looped around the block and began to follow him. It wasn't easy to trail a man on foot and not be noticed, but Eric seemed to be in a daze. They pulled ahead of him and parked on the opposite side of the street and watched him walk past the car. They repeated the maneuver at least six times all the way to the end of California Street and back.

"The guy must be crazy. It's cold out here and he takes a two and a half hour walk? Something's wrong."

"She's messed up his brain."

"Yeah, it looks like she dumped him, not the other way around."

"We should talk to him. Maybe he'll tell us what's going on."

"Let's do it tomorrow, I'm beat. I bet he is too."

"Tomorrow sounds good to me."

Mary had spent a half an hour sitting in her living room staring at the door after Eric left. Her cheeks were wet from her tears. He had acted as she suspected he would. She had turned his love for her into hate. When she accepted the fact that he was gone for good, she stood up, wiped her face and went to the bedroom to turn on her computer. She looked, but couldn't find any messages. She sent one:

Eric Wing and I are no longer together. The CSA has no proof of wrongdoing. This assignment should be aborted, and I should return to my real life.

She shut down her computer and went to bed.

Eric had never been late for work before and Angel was concerned. It also bothered her that two CSA agents were sitting in the outer office across from her desk.

"I don't understand it. Mr. Wing has never been late before."

"We're familiar with Mr. Wing's routine. Perhaps you could call him and let him know that we are waiting."

"You say you are familiar with his routine. Have you been watching him? Is he in trouble?"

"We'd appreciate it if you could make the call."

Eric arrived as Angel was dialing the number. She put the phone down and introduced the two agents. Eric ushered them into his office and closed the door.

"How can I help you gentlemen?"

"Let's not start from scratch, Mr. Wing. We know about your relationship with Mary Chang and we suspect that she probably already told you about us. Hasn't she?"

"As a matter of fact she has. She also said that you didn't have any evidence against her. If you had, you'd have already arrested her."

"That's true. We tried to enlist her help to turn on her employers using her relationship with you as leverage. But judging from your actions last night and this morning, you two no longer have a relationship."

"What are you talking about? Have you been

following me?"

"We've been monitoring her and we stumbled onto you last night as you left her place. Nearly a three hour walk in the cold, I'm surprised that you're not sick this morning."

"Why are you here?"

"We want to try to get your help."

"Help doing what?"

"We want you to reconcile with Ms. Chang and find out what she is after and maybe provide some misinformation to her employers."

"You want me to turn on her, don't you?"

"Didn't she turn on you and deceive you from the very beginning?"

"Before I decide if I'm going to help you, I want to know everything about your investigation and everything you know about Mary."

"I'm sure you know almost everything already, but we'll tell you what we know."

Eric and Agents Morris and Coleman spent the next half hour reviewing all the information related to their investigation and Mary Chang's dossier. Eric told them about his discussion with Mary and that she said that she loved him. She also left it up to him if they were going to stay together or not. After the exchange on the topics of love, betrayal, duty and country, Eric agreed to work with the CSA.

After the agents left, Eric had second thoughts. He wanted to hurt Mary more than he cared about doing his duty. None of it made sense to him. Universal was going to manufacture robots in China. The technology involved was already being used by several other companies and it was readily available on the internet. It was not worth a spy's time. Eric spent part of the day convincing Angel that everything was fine and there was nothing to worry about. He also had to convince himself to go through with the agreement he made with the CSA. Eric was reluctant to admit it, but he was afraid of Mary. He was mad at her but he knew deep down that he still loved her. He didn't know if he could ever really turn against her.

Mary went through her work day on automatic pilot. There was a staff meeting with Charles, but she didn't need to contribute anything. There were phone calls with her counterparts at Universal. She ate lunch alone. She wrote two memos and a client letter and the work day was done. She was getting resigned to the fact that she would soon be leaving this life behind. She'd be back at the wharf waiting tables. She would miss Eric and her apartment and having all the money she needed, but the problems would also disappear with the perks.

She rode the bus home in good spirits, trying to capture all the sights and sounds of this life before they were lost to her. She thought about how good it would be to see her mom and dad again even with their meddling and criticism of her lifestyle. She stopped at the grocery store to buy a few things for dinner and she used the payphone to call the answering service to give her parents the all clear message. She was singing a song by Sly and the Family Stone when she entered the apartment.

After cooking and eating dinner, she turned on her computer and looked for a response to her last message. She found it:

Repair your relationship and cooperate with the CSA.

She was sorry that she had just eaten. She felt like she was going to throw up. She and Eric were finished. The way he left told her that he was done. They were asking the impossible. She was hugging herself, rocking back and forth, when the phone rang.

"Hello."

"Mary, we're still a couple."

"Eric, are you crazy? I can't believe you still want me. You're risking everything."

"Do you love me?"

"Yes, but..."

"Can I come over?"

"No, not yet. I need to think."

"I need you."

"Tomorrow, we'll meet tomorrow. Eric, are you sure?"

"Yes, I'm sure."

"Okay, we'll meet tomorrow for lunch. I want to talk about this in a public place. Mangia Tutti on Clay at one o'clock."

"I'll be there. I love you."

"I love you too, Eric."

Mary put the phone down and she sat quietly thinking. She wanted him to end it and walk away. She was happy that he still wanted her, but she felt that she had to convince him to let her go. She wanted him, but she also wanted him to be safe and happy. She'd try to reason with him tomorrow.

Mary went back to her computer and began to type.

> **I cannot continue this assignment. Mr. Wing has ended our relationship irrevocably. He is of limited value. I will not work with the CSA. If I am not reassigned, I will terminate our arrangement.**

Mary reread her message then sent it. She had made up her mind. She was going to save Eric and try to get back to her old life. If Beijing didn't agree, she would run and hide. It wasn't as if she was a real spy, she was nothing, an errand girl. It wouldn't be worth their effort to come after her. Her computer signaled an incoming message had arrived. As she read it, she turned pale.

> **In your absence, your parents accepted our invitation to visit their homeland. Their many relatives have been pleased to see them again. They are having a wonderful time. They are scheduled to return to the United States next week, but I fear that there will be a problem with their passports that will delay their return. Before your parents' problems escalate, repair your relationship and cooperate with the CSA.**

Mary's eyes filled with tears and the computer screen became a blur. She lay down on the bed and cried, uncontrollably. She felt helpless and hopeless and she cried most of the night. She had no choice now, she had to work with the CSA. She thought about it and decided not to tell the CSA that Beijing directed her to cooperate. Neither the CSA nor Eric needed to know that.

Eric was relieved to have finished talking to Mary. He was afraid that his anger toward her would spill into the conversation, so he kept his sentences short and he concentrated on his breathing. The CSA had told him to make nice with her and he did. The CSA told him that she was using him and he was beginning to believe them. She had him so confused. She kept lying to him and pushing him away. He was a mess and he had to get himself together before they met for lunch.

He called Agent Morris' number.

"Hello, Commerce Security Agency, San Francisco Office. This is Agent Morris, how can I help you?"

"Agent Morris, this is Eric Wing. I called Mary like you asked. We're going to have lunch tomorrow. "

"Good, get back together as soon as you can. You are our leverage to get her to work with us."

Eric cringed at the thought that he was going to be using her. "I'll make up with her. I want to ring her neck, but I won't."

"Just relax, I know you have feelings for her and you probably feel betrayed. I don't think she's a bad guy. Take it easy; give her a chance."

"I'll let you know how it goes."

"Good luck, Mr. Wing."

Eric hung up. He felt better after talking tough about Mary to the CSA. He still wasn't sure whether or not he'd cave when he saw her again. He wouldn't mind putting her through hell as long as she ended up in his arms after he had his revenge. He couldn't wait to put his problems with Mary behind him, but he still had a job to do.

While work was being done on the China manufacturing move, Eric had been off-loading most of his domestic responsibilities. His division supported the engineering group when they needed prototypes built for military applications. One of Eric's transition team managers, Larry Murray, was directly responsible for engineering support among his other duties. Eric had scheduled a meeting with Larry and his staff to review the engineering support group's projects that were being off-loaded.

Scheduling the meeting late in the workday was a mistake. Each member of Larry's team was committed to his project and had developed detailed presentations on each one. Eric was able to pay close attention to the first four presentations, but the level of detail and the technical jargon was overwhelming. He almost drifted off to sleep several times. He was just about to suggest that they end the meeting and pick it up again in the morning when he heard the presenter say that the system's tracking ability was more than an order of magnitude above the currently available systems.

Eric looked at the handout he had been given that summarized the presentation. The detection system being presented was designed to detect shock waves from sonic displacement emissions. The previous accurate range of similar devices was 500 feet. The new device could detect signals from over 2000 yards away. This device could be of immediate use to combat troops to detect the location of sniper fire.

He was sure that the military would be interested. He was also sure that the Chinese would be interested. Eric was a valued target after all, and it appeared that the Chinese knew it before he did. There had to be a leak somewhere inside

Universal.

Eric abruptly ended the meeting. He had to tell the CSA what he suspected. He also needed to know if Mary already knew what the Chinese wanted from him. He didn't trust her yet. But regardless of what Mary knew or wanted, she could never get him to betray his country or his company.

It was late, but he called agent Morris anyway. The phone rang four times before a groggy sounding Morris answered it.

"This is Morris, who's calling?"

"Agent Morris, this is Eric Wing again. I just found out what the Chinese are interested in."

"What is it?"

"It's a sound detection tracking system that we have in development."

"What's so special about the system?"

"It can recognize and lock in on the source of an intense sound emission from a mile away and provide real time firing coordinates to an infantryman or a drone. The tracking system is accurate within inches of the target. That means reduced collateral damage, just what the military is looking for. Only the target need be destroyed."

"Wow, the military would love to get their hands on something like that."

"So would our allies and enemies."

"So that's what she's after. Why didn't you tell me about this before?"

"I just found out about it myself."

"But apparently, the Chinese knew about it, ever since

they arranged for you and Mary to get together. Maybe Mary isn't as innocent as she claims to be."

"I still believe Mary doesn't know what Beijing is after and I wonder what she will do when she finds out."

"It's obvious that the research has already been compromised since the Chinese know about it. The first thing that needs to be done is to secure the project and the project plans. The research team will have to be investigated to find the security leak. What's the project called?"

"The project is called 'Pinpoint'."

"I will contact the necessary people at Homeland Security. Go ahead with your meeting with Mary and let me know what happens."

"Okay, I'll call you tomorrow. Goodnight."

Eric was more worried about Mary than ever. He prayed that she was just a pawn and hadn't been a party to the plot all along. The idea of getting revenge was forgotten. He wanted her back and he wanted to be able to trust her. He had no doubt that if she failed to convince him or the CSA, she would be hung out to dry. He was exhausted, so he packed up and left the office, anticipating another sleepless night.

Mary woke up early and was horrified at the way she looked in the mirror. She worked at reducing the puffiness under her eyes with marginal success. She put on a frilly blue blouse and a straight black skirt. She looked feminine and vulnerable, just the look she was going for. She wanted Eric back and now that her parents' lives hung in the balance, she was going to use everything she had to get him back.

She expected the luncheon date to be awkward, and it was. Mary greeted him with a kiss on the cheek, which wasn't accepted with enthusiasm. Eric was closemouthed and grim looking. She tried small talk, but Eric didn't expend any effort to making it work. Mary sat back in her chair.

"You asked for this meeting, and now you don't want to talk to me. What's going on?"

"I'm sorry; I don't know what to say."

"On the phone, you said we were a couple. Do you love me?"

"Yes, I do."

"You don't sound too convincing. But I guess we'll have time to prove ourselves later. As I told you, I was directed to get close to you. I don't know why yet, but I'll be told when I need to know. If we're together, I'll be pressured into working with the CSA. Are you with me so far?"

"Yes, I'm with you."

"If the CSA grants me immunity, I'll cooperate with them. If I'm found out by the Chinese, me and everyone I know and love will be in danger. Do you understand?"

"Yes, I do."

"We're both risking a lot for a roll in the hay, if that's all it is."

"It's more than that. I love you more than I can say."

"All right, my love, we're a couple. I know that you're mad at me. Believe me, I'll make it up to you. Let's spend the rest of the day together."

"I can't, I've got too much to do."

"I suppose that you've got to check in with Agent

Morris?"

"Yes, I do. How did you know that Morris contacted me?"

Mary smiled. "That's what I'd do if I were him. You were his only leverage. He had to get us back together to force me to work with him. So he appealed to your sense of duty to get you to help him."

Eric was flustered. "I didn't do it because of a sense of duty. I wanted you back and this seemed like the only way that we would have a chance."

"You need to understand that he has a job to do. He doesn't care about either of us. He just wants to get the job done."

"I know it."

"Just keep it in mind. You will have to trust one of us. It should be me."

"I trust you."

"No, you don't. I believe you love me, but you don't trust me. I can see it and feel it. You weren't going to tell me that you talked to Agent Morris, were you?"

"No, I guess not."

"Well, you'd better decide if you are going to trust me soon. The game we are about to play is serious and we need to be able to trust each other."

"I want to trust you, but we didn't exactly start out on the right foot, did we?"

"No we didn't. But if we are going to be together, it has to be us against everyone else. Can't you see that?"

"Yes. I'll get on board, but don't ever let me down

again."

"I never will. Now let's eat something then go somewhere quiet and call Agent Morris together."

After lunch, they left the restaurant and walked down Clay to Transamerica Redwood Park. Eric pulled out his phone.

"What should we tell him?"

"The truth, we're back together and we will work with him if we're guaranteed immunity."

"Immunity from what?"

"From anything we've done or anything we're going to have to do."

Eric dialed the number and touched the speakerphone button.

"This is Agent Morris."

"Mary and I are back together and we'll both work with you if you agree to grant us immunity."

"Okay, we'll work something out."

Mary took the phone. "We want the agreement in writing before we do anything."

"Oh, both of you are on the line. You really are back together."

"That's right, and as soon as this call is over, I'm going to remind Eric of the advantages of being together." The remark got a smile from Eric.

Morris ignored the attempt at humor and said, "I'll have an agreement drawn up and get back to you." Morris hung up.

Eric was surprised that the call ended abruptly. "He

didn't seem too happy."

"He was probably pissed that we called him together. Now he knows that he can't play us against each other."

"You mentioned something about reminding me of the advantages of being together. I find that I am free for the rest of the day after all. Let's go to my place."

"Great idea, I could use a little down time, no pun intended."

CHAPTER TWELVE

Morris and Coleman were parked across the street and they had trailed the couple as they left the restaurant and walked to the park holding hands. They seemed happy. The agents watched them make the phone call and then hail a cab.

"We might as well return to the office and try to get the attorneys to draft an immunity agreement. What those two are about to do isn't against the law. At least, not in this state."

"We'll have to have a review done of all military projects and research activities being done at Universal. They also need to determine which projects and activities are under Wing's control or that he has access to."

"Do you think she's going to work with us on the up and up?"

"I don't know; I don't trust her. She may have been loyal to this country all along. I doubt that Wing's wang caused her to change sides."

Coleman laughed at the rare joke made by Morris.

"If she isn't on the up and up, we could end up wasting a lot of time."

"I know. We'll give it a couple of months. After that, we'll get Wing replaced and we'll see if Mary stands by her man when he's no longer valuable to the Chinese."

Eric and Mary made up for most of the afternoon and early evening. When they were done, she told him her life story. It didn't make for a good spy novel. According to her, she was the Chinese version of a rebellious teenage girl; she got B's instead of A's. Working for the Chinese was more of a family tradition than an ideological choice. As far as she was concerned, she just ran errands for her father. When he retired, she took her direction from a guy on the Internet. This was her first real assignment with a change of identity and an up close and personal target. Then she told him that she had been directed to make up with him and cooperate with the CSA.

"Is that why we made up, because you were directed to?"

"Yes, I wanted to keep you safe by getting out of your life, but the CSA and Beijing wanted us to stay together."

"Didn't you want us to be together?"

"Of course I did, but I also wanted you out of this mess. There's one more thing I need to tell you. My parents went to China for a visit and they won't be allowed to return here unless I do what I'm told."

"So you had no choice but to come back to me."

"That's right, I had no choice. But it's what I wanted to do."

"Somehow, I'm not reassured that I'm the irresistible hunk that I think I am."

"I've been trying to reassure you all afternoon. Let's put your ego aside for the time being. I think my parents will be all right since I've done everything that I've been asked to do. What bothers me is that I don't know what Beijing wants from you. Do you have anything that you think they might want?"

"Well, I'm a very important man. I oversee a lot of important projects at Universal."

"Are you still working on your ego?"

"No, seriously, it could be any number of things. I guess we'll just have to wait until they ask."

"Eric, you can see that I have a whole lot on my plate right now."

"Yes I certainly can."

"I need you to trust me and stand by me. If it gets to be too much for you, tell me. I'll understand and I'll get out of your life forever."

"I'll do whatever needs to be done."

"You know that it works the other way too."

"What do you mean?"

"If you stand by me and we get through this, I'll never let you go."

"That sounds good to me."

Eric took her in his arms and kissed her like he meant it. With their problems identified and their course of action agreed upon, there was really no reason for Eric to stay. He tried to make her think that he was comfortable hanging around the apartment making small talk, but she could see that he was anxious to get back to work, so she let him go.

After he left, Mary turned on her computer and sent a message.

I have done what was asked of me. I've reconciled with Mr. Wing and I have agreed to work

with the CSA. I look forward to my parents' safe return.

She read the message several times. She was tempted to use Eric's first name but Mr. Wing made her seem more detached, so she didn't make the change.

At ten o'clock the following morning, Agent Morris had the immunity agreement in hand and he and Coleman were heading to the Montgomery Group's offices to hand it over to Mary.

"Do you think she has anything we can use?"

"No." Morris shook his head. "We're betting on the come."

"What?"

"We're betting that she will have something useful in the near future. Don't you gamble?"

"No, I don't. It's a bad idea for CSA agents to gamble."

"Whether you do or not, it's a good idea to be familiar with the language in case you have to talk to gamblers or drug dealers."

"We're not vice cops."

"The more you know, the better agent you'll be."

Coleman checked his watch. It was only 10:15 AM and he was already annoyed with Morris. *"Christ, this is going to be a long day."*

Mary was in a good mood in spite of her concern for her parents. In her mind, once they were safely back home, all her problems would be solved. She wouldn't have to betray

Eric or her country.

At the office, she had recently been assigned to a new client, Sanford Foods, which operated a chain of fast food restaurants. The company was expanding to Asia, and the approach they were planning to use was to buy a number of existing restaurants and turn them into Sanford sites. Charles had put a team together weeks ago to work with Sanford, but now at the eleventh hour, he was adding Mary to the team.

Mary was worried that moving from the Universal account would limit her access to Eric and disturb her Beijing handler. She, of course, had access most nights and she thought that there wouldn't be a problem. She was right. What she didn't expect was that Sanford was moving at record pace and they wanted to take the team on their first Asian trip immediately. Stops were planned in Shanghai and Beijing. When she heard about the trip, she went to Charles and tried to beg off. Charles told her that she had been asked for by name.

Mary went back to her desk to call Eric and she found that there were two salesmen waiting to talk to her. She said that she would give them a few minutes and the secretary ushered them into her office.

"Mr. Morris and Mr. Coleman, what can I do for you?" She offered them a seat as she closed the office door.

"Here's the agreement you asked for." Morris handed an envelope to her and sat back down. Mary opened it and took her time reading it. She smiled and said, "Very good. It's exactly what I wanted. What I like most about it is that I'm not required to provide information leading to the prosecution or conviction of anyone. I'm only required to be forthcoming and truthful. I will be. I'll tell you everything I know, but I doubt it will help you."

"We'll see. We're going to need to debrief you."

"We'd better make it soon. I've just been told that I've got another China trip to make in a few days."

"Is it a trip for business or government work?"

"These days, I'm not sure there's a difference."

Morris nodded knowingly and grinned.

Mary added, "The trip isn't for Universal, I've been given another client, Sanford Foods."

"What? Get out of it."

"I've tried. No luck. It doesn't seem to matter. I still have access to Eric and according to my instructions, Eric is my assignment, not Universal."

"Maybe you have been taken out of play."

"Fine by me."

"It's not fine by us."

"Maybe this is part of the grand plan they have for me. I was told that the new client asked for me by name."

"They probably asked for the hot chick in the office on the left. Find out if you were really asked for and why. Make sure this is a legitimate move and not Charles Tong giving the customer some eye candy."

"Okay, I'll talk to him again. You guys need to think about the possibility that you just lost a double agent."

"We'll see. Meanwhile, why don't you drop by our office after work and we'll debrief you just in case your reassignment falls through."

"That's not a good idea. I'm being watched. My handler knows where I am and what I do. I can't drop by the CSA offices."

"Okay, we'll arrange something. You need to see what you can do to get back on the Universal account."

"All right, I'll try. If there's nothing else, you gentlemen have a nice day."

Mary waited until they left and called Eric. He was in a meeting and she left a message to get a return call. There was a possibility that the new client wanted a pretty face on the team. She knew that businessmen could be jerks just like everybody else, maybe more so. She was tempted to go back to Charles, but she decided to wait until the next time he called her in for a chat. She was hoping that her handler was behind her move to a new client and that he was putting her on the shelf so she would have nothing for the CSA. Then she and Eric would be left alone.

Eric's meeting was with the Chairman and CEO Ralph Petersen. Eric was reviewing the implications of the tracking system for military application. He told Petersen that the military would pay dearly for a system that could quickly identify and locate a sniper.

Petersen was elated. With the way wars were being fought, a system like this would be invaluable. This project could be bigger than the China move and have immediate returns.

"A project like this needs high level management supervision. We may need to reorganize to provide the necessary resources and focus on this project's needs. The China project will take another three to five years to complete and turn profitable. Project Pinpoint will be profitable a lot sooner. I'll leave it up to you. How soon do you want to move up the ladder? Which project do you want to be responsible for?"

"I'll take Pinpoint."

"Good choice. The full board will need to see a presentation in short order."

"I'll put it together with proposed schedules and potential profit estimates."

"Excellent!"

The meeting broke up and Eric had to forgo the after meeting schmoozing and get back to his office and get started on his new assignment. He was excited. He couldn't see the downside unless the project failed, but the technology was solid. Now he didn't have to spend two years in China, he didn't have to replace Angel and he was on a faster track up the ladder. Then he remembered the spy who loved him and the CSA. When the CSA and the military learned about project Pinpoint, they wouldn't allow him and Mary to be in the same zip code.

He checked his messages and returned Mary's call.

"Hello, Mary, I'm returning your call. Is everything alright?"

"No, they've taken me off the Universal account and put me on Sanford Foods. Sanford is expanding to Asia and I'll be traveling for weeks at a time. Maybe you can have a word with Charles."

"I don't think I can do that. I'm no longer on the China project myself. I've been moved to a new top secret project."

"Oh, no. Now you are a valuable target, aren't you?"

"Yes. Now there is no way they'll let us work together. They might not let us be together at all."

"Can you refuse to take the new project?"

"I asked for it."

"I don't understand. You asked for a project that

would split us up?"

"No, I mean yes. I wasn't thinking that far ahead. We don't know what the agencies will say. This project may be the bait that the CSA wants to use. Let's sit down with them and talk it out and see where we stand."

"I'm afraid that I'll find out that you want this project more than you want me."

"That's not the way it is."

"I hope not."

"If we don't like what we hear from the CSA, we can refuse to cooperate and you can quit Montgomery and you can go back to your old life with a new fiancé."

"That sounds fine, except for the fact that my parents are in China and we would be on our own."

"The CSA would still have to protect me and my family to make sure that a top secret project isn't compromised," said Eric.

"Am I part of that family that would be getting protection?"

"Absolutely, you and your parents."

"I wonder if the CSA will agree with that."

"We'll talk more about it once your parents are safely back home. Until then, we'll play nice with everybody."

"The CSA is arranging to debrief me; I want you there with me."

"Okay, let me know where and when. I've got to get back to work."

"I love you. Bye"

When Eric put the phone down, he paused to think

about what Mary said about choosing the project over her. He hadn't. But what was worse, he hadn't given Mary a thought when he decided to choose Pinpoint. Consciously, Mary was more important to him than any project, but he gave no thought to her when the choice was being made. It bothered him and he knew it bothered her.

Mary felt happy and uneasy. She had just received an informal proposal of marriage and she took it in stride. No squeals or shrieks or screams. She couldn't put her finger on the source of the uneasiness, but it had to be something that Eric said. She dismissed her search for the problem and decided to enjoy her new status as fiancée to be.

She wondered what life would be like if all she had to do was to make Eric happy. No spying, no CSA, no handler, just a husband to take care of. They would be able to start a family. It would be a dream come true. But first, she had to take care of the family she already had.

She decided not to bother Charles about the change in assignments. It didn't matter. Anyway, Eric was no longer on the China project. Sanford Foods would get her to China if she had to go and get her parents out by herself.

The more she thought about her Mom and Dad, the more nervous she got. She decided to go home, her real home and get her address book. She would call her relatives near Beijing and track down her parents.

She waited for the workday to end. Now she had a plan of action. At 4:45, Agent Morris called about the debriefing. Mary was to make a doctor's appointment for 11:00 AM the following morning. Morris told her the name and location of the doctor and said the appointment would last forty-five minutes.

With the workday finally over, she headed to her

apartment to pick up her house keys. She got the keys and changed her clothes. She dressed casually so as not to stand out as she walked through her old neighborhood. Her old home was ten minutes and a world away from her apartment. She found at least a week's worth of mail and newspapers piled up in the doorway. She gathered everything up and opened the door. The place was the same. A few months away hadn't made any difference.

She went into her room. It too was the same except it was cleaner than the way she left it. She looked around the room; it looked like it belonged to a teenager. When she was here, she felt like a teenager. She knew that if she ever returned to this life, it wouldn't be as a teen. She found her address book and put it in her purse. She went to the living room and took a book from the shelf. She opened it and took out a note left by her father. She didn't want to take the time to read it. She wanted to get out of there as soon as she could. She took one last look around and noted the hospital corners on her parent's bed. It was not the way her mother would make it. She left quickly and took a detour on the way to the apartment to see if she was being followed.

On the way to the apartment, she called Eric and told him about the doctor's appointment and asked him to meet her there. He said he would. Once she got home and stepped inside the apartment, she pulled out her father's note and read it. She felt her knees buckle and she made her way to the couch. She reread the note.

Daughter, your mother and I have gone on a trip to our homeland. I hoped you would have come home in time to talk to us face to face. We do not plan to return to this country. We are old and tired and wish to spend our remaining time with friends and family in familiar surroundings. We would have taken you with us if that was your choice. We have transferred funds enough to ensure our comfort. The house and the remaining funds are yours. We would love for you to join us. I know that you are a product of this country. We wish you well. Take care of yourself.

She howled and began crying. After a few minutes, she stopped and struggled to pull herself together. Her handler had given her the impression that he had intervened and prevented her parent's return. They had not planned to return. The handler was jerking her around. She became furious for a moment, then calmed down a bit to collect her thoughts.

She reached in her purse and got the address book. She looked through the address book and found her Aunt's address and number. She hesitated. Now that she knew that her parents were in China by choice, there was no urgency to contact them. She was curious to see what her handler would say to her when her parents stayed there week after week. Would he try to frighten her and coerce her into doing something stupid? She already hated her handler and the people he worked for; now that hatred intensified with every new piece of information she gathered.

She was beginning to have her doubts about everyone in her life. Her parents got her into this mess in the first place, Eric appeared to have fallen in love with his new project and the CSA just wanted to do their job. She had to look out for herself. She turned on her computer to look for new messages. There were none. She typed:

The CSA will debrief me tomorrow. Shall I be accurate and truthful? Are my parents returning home soon?

She sent the message and went to the kitchen to make dinner. She hoped working in the kitchen would distract her and pass the time until she got an answer to her message. It was 6 PM in San Francisco and 10 AM in Beijing. She thought her handler would be at his desk. She expected an immediate reply.

She hadn't thought about it before, but it almost always had taken hours to receive responses no matter what time of day she sent messages. That seemed to indicate that her handler was of low rank and had to have his work reviewed before he could contact her. It could also indicate that she was not that important an asset. She wondered if she wasn't just a decoy. She thought about offering that idea to the CSA during her debriefing.

The phone rang and Mary glanced at the clock as she went to answer it. It was 6:15 and she thought it was probably Eric looking for a meal and some dessert.

"Hi Babe, what's cooking?"

"Nothing, I was going to put something together, but now I've got a better idea. You feed me."

"What's the matter, you mad at me?"

"No, just annoyed. But it's nothing that a free meal wouldn't fix."

"Do you want to go out, or should I bring something?"

"Bring something."

"I'll be there in an hour. Love you."

"You better bring something good."

Mary hung up smiling. She wasn't going to fight with him over his new love interest. She was just going to make sure that he knew there were consequences to not giving her enough attention. She loved him and she wasn't going to rock the boat until after there was some paper between them. She went to the bedroom to watch some TV before her dinner was delivered.

Agents Morris and Coleman were working late. They received information from their people monitoring passport usage and security that Mr. and Mrs. Simon Chang had left the US for China ten days ago. They were scheduled to return after seven days, but they hadn't reentered the country.

"As far as we know, the old man retired years ago. He was never a major player. He was more of an errand boy. It made more sense to watch him than to arrest him. That's why we left him alone. The agency never tried to turn him because he wasn't important enough."

"So the old man takes his wife and goes home for a visit and they hold on to him."

"We don't know that yet. Maybe he got sick or just decided to extend their stay."

"It's more likely that they are being held to use as leverage to make Mary do what she's told."

"I guess Beijing doesn't trust her."

"Too bad, she might have been legitimate before this, but now that they have her parents, we can't trust her either."

"Let's see how the debriefing goes. She may come clean and tell us that her parents are being held."

"Either way, we need to bug both her and the boyfriend's apartments and phones. Let's also contact the military and have them beef up the security protocols on all top-secret projects at Universal. That will make sure the boyfriend can't get anything sensitive in or out of the building."

"Good idea. Now, let's go home."

Mary wasn't looking forward to the debriefing especially after Eric called and told her that he was tied up and couldn't go with her. She was pissed. He had plenty of time to spend with her last night, but now, when she needed him, he was tied up. She had to put her emotions aside for now and deal with the CSA. She'd deal with Eric later.

The address she was given was for a medical office building on Gough Street near Pine. She entered the lobby and looked at the directory. She found the doctor's name and took the elevator to the second floor. The office looked as she suspected it would. There was a receptionist and patients seated, waiting with their magazines and media players. She identified herself to the receptionist and was asked to take a seat. After a few minutes, a nurse came into the waiting area and called her name. Mary followed the nurse to an examining room. She opened the door to reveal Agents Morris, Coleman and a person who appeared to be a technician. They were sitting around a table on which they had a polygraph machine.

"Is that necessary?"

"I'm afraid it is. We need to be sure that you are on our team."

"Apparently you don't trust me, so why should I trust you?"

"We don't care if you trust us or not. We do want you

to be truthful with us. Work with us and lead us to the people threatening our nation and we'll leave you, your boyfriend and your parents alone."

"Cut the crap, I don't know anybody who's threatening our nation. I've been associated with people who steal company secrets and ideas. There's nothing more to it."

"If that's your view of things, fine, but we are going to find out everything you know and we're using the polygraph."

"Okay, let's get on with it."

For the next half hour, Mary answered their questions, and she told them everything she could about working with her contact. They were especially interested in her face to face contact with her handler, Hui Kai. She told them that she had only seen Hui Kai briefly. They asked for a description. Mary's description surprised them by its level of detail. Mary explained that she was good with faces. Morris got his laptop and started the CSA's facial reconstruction program. Morris told her that the bureau had experts who sketch subjects and use computer aids to create a likeness. They also had software for use in the field. With Mary's description, Morris was able to develop a good likeness of Hui Kai.

"When you were in China, did you meet any other people working with your handler?"

"No, he was alone."

"Maybe the people you met there on the other team were agents?"

"It's possible, but there's no way of knowing."

"Maybe there is." Morris turned his laptop toward Mary. "I'm going to show you a number of agents working for the Chinese. There are about ten people we are especially interested in."

Mary looked at the pictures. "No, no, none of these people were in our meetings." She paused at one picture. "You guys are still playing games with me. I thought the polygraph was enough. Now you're trying to trick me."

"What are you talking about?"

"I saw this guy before, but not in China. He was at the airport. He was in the shuttle with me on the ride from the airport to the city."

"Are you sure?"

"Yes, positive."

Mary had pointed out the picture of Dr. Jiang Wang, head of the Office of Business Operations, Beijing, China.

"Did he say anything? Where did he get dropped off?"

"No, he didn't say anything to me. I wasn't paying attention. I was upset. I had just been blindsided by the CSA."

"Did you see where he was dropped off?"

"I got dropped off first."

Morris and Coleman were visibly excited. They both got up and paced around the room. The technician looked confused. "What's wrong?" Mary asked.

Morris said, "The man you pointed out is a very important man. He's very high up in the pecking order."

"I came back from China over two months ago and you've just found out that a top spy is here. It looks like the No Fly List process isn't working."

"Save the sarcasm; we found you, didn't we?"

Morris and Coleman walked to the other side of the

room and began whispering. They talked for a minute, and then Coleman took out his cell phone and left the room as he dialed. Morris continued with the debriefing.

"We are obviously interested in this man and his movements while he was in this country, but we think that it was just a coincidence that he was on your shuttle."

"You think it was a coincidence that two Chinese agents happened to be on the same airport shuttle?"

"The man you picked out isn't an agent; he's more of a manager."

"Could he have been managing the operation that I'm involved in?"

"No, not directly, he's too high up for that. Odds are, he was here to attend some seminar or something. Let's get back to your activities."

The meeting lasted another quarter hour. Morris repeated questions that had already been answered. As Mary was leaving, Morris said, "When you go to China on your new assignment, we'll need you to do a few things for us. I'll tell you the details later."

"Are you trying to upset me? What things do you want me to do?"

"It's nothing dangerous or difficult. I just want you to make a drop and a pickup. You'll be perfectly safe."

"I don't like this."

"Trust me, it's no big deal."

"I trust you just like you trust me."

CHAPTER THIRTEEN

The next few days passed quietly. Mary had told Eric that she was disappointed that he wasn't with her for the CSA debriefing. She had been calm and controlled. He told her that he had to make a presentation to the board of directors. She appeared to accept his apology and his excuse, but something about the way she acted told Eric that he had made a huge mistake and he had better not make another.

He felt like he was on probation, and he knew it was a bad time for her to be going away for at least three weeks. He was happy that he would have the time to concentrate on work, but he wished that they were on better terms. His uneasiness with their relationship made him work hard at putting this latest gaffe behind them. He cooked for her and bought her a diamond tennis bracelet. She refused it at first saying it would just be a reminder of how he wasn't there for her when she needed him. That night Eric outdid himself in the bedroom. In the morning, she put on the bracelet and said that it would be a reminder of a different event.

Jade, Mr. Tong's secretary, made the travel arrangements for Tong, Mary and the Sanford Foods team. There were two stops planned: Shanghai and Beijing, two of the ten most populous cities in China. Charles Tong had used his contacts to make inroads with the government. The Sanford team was to set the groundwork for the purchase of an existing restaurant chain with locations in each of the cities and several stand alone businesses that would supply the chain.

The Sanford team had made similar moves in Australia and Latin America. The Montgomery Group was to help with government and cultural issues and protocols. Charles and Mary simply had to help negotiate terms of sale for any restaurants that Sanford wanted to buy. Charles thought it would be a piece of cake. Mary asked him again why she was chosen to take the trip and Charles admitted that she would be interpreting for the client and she would be a pleasant interface between Sanford and the Chinese restaurateurs. Ordinarily, Mary would have been upset and given Charles flack, but she was promised time off to meet with her parents when they were in Beijing.

Mary had met with Agent Morris on the bus ride home after work, the day she was debriefed. He gave her an encrypted thumb drive and told her to give it to a man who identified himself as Mr. Chin. He showed her a picture of Chin. She was supposed to get a replacement drive from Chin and bring it back home. If she couldn't make contact with Chin, she was supposed to return the drive to Morris. She thought it was stupid for Morris to meet her on the bus, but since she had been ordered to cooperate with the CSA, it didn't matter if she was seen with him.

The trip was scheduled for Monday. On Friday, it hit Eric that Mary would be gone for three weeks, maybe more. He left work Friday night and went to her apartment and didn't leave her side. When she went to the kitchen to cook, he followed her. He passed up a Raider game on TV to sit and talk with her after dinner. He even tried to shower with her before bed. She chased him out of the bathroom, pretending to be pissed, but she loved the attention. It turned out to be a wonderful weekend. Eric did everything he could to ensure that she'd miss him while she was away.

On Monday, he rented a car and took her to the airport. She made him drop her at the terminal. She didn't want him to come inside. He made sure to tell her that he loved her and she walked away, careful not to let him see her tears. By the time she made it through security and reached the gate, she had pulled herself together. She didn't expect it to be a good flight; she was sitting next to Charles all the way.

The drive back to the city seemed a lot longer than usual to Eric. With time to think, he took inventory of all the obstacles that needed to be overcome to hold on to Mary. He knew that the CSA had eliminated one. With the security protocols they had requested that the military put on Project Pinpoint, there was no way any information could be stolen. Even with Eric's full cooperation, Mary couldn't breach the project.

Eric's mind wandered between Mary and the project until he reached the rental agency to turn in the car. He was sure he had done all he could to show her that he was worth coming back to. He went to the office determined to bury himself in his work until she came home.

Morris and Coleman were at the airport watching Mary board.

"What did you put on the drive?"

"I had the instruction manual for my digital camera encrypted."

"Why'd you do that? If they intercept it and read the file, they'll know that we're not taking her seriously."

"The combination of the bad English in the original manual and the encryption will make it impossible to read."

"What about Chin?"

"There is no Chin. She's not legitimate and I'm going

to prove it. When she returns the drive, we'll be able to tell if they attempted to read it."

"Why are you so sure that she's not being straight with us?"

"Of all the pictures we showed her at the debriefing, she picks out the one guy not on our hit list. She's not going to give us anything useful. Either she's playing us, or the other side is using her just like we plan to do."

"I disagree; I think she's trying to do the right thing now."

"You're a sucker for a pretty face."

"We'll see who the better judge of character is; I think your digital camera's secrets are safe."

The first stop on the trip was Shanghai. Even though Mary was preoccupied with getting in and out of the city as quickly as possible in order to find her parents in or near Beijing, she found a lot to like about Shanghai. It had the speed of New York in the commercial areas and cultural charm in areas scattered throughout the city. She was thankful that Charles skipped the tourist locations and stuck to business. He was trying to gauge the client. His process was to concentrate on work first. If the client wanted to mix business with pleasure, he had to say so.

They reached the hotel at 5:00 PM local time, and Charles had scheduled a meeting for 8:00 AM the next morning.

At the morning meeting, everyone who had made the trip looked like they were hung over, but the Sanford people held their own. The meeting went well and the groundwork was laid for subsequent meetings. There was an exchange of gifts and plans were made for dinner at a gentlemen's club. Mary and Pat, the woman member of the Sanford team, had a pleasant dinner in the hotel restaurant. Mary got back to her room at 9:00 PM and she checked her computer for instructions from either of her masters. There was nothing from the CSA, but Hui Kai had replied to her message from four days ago.

We understood that the CSA would be debriefing you when you agreed to work for them. We assumed you knew enough to tell them the truth without having been instructed to do so. As for your parents, they are having a wonderful time here and they have chosen not to leave anytime soon.

If the CSA has given you an assignment, complete it. You must establish your credibility with them. Help them in any way you can.

Mary looked at the message and tried to understand it. She read what it said, and thought about what it didn't say. There was no mention of Eric and his new project. There was no mention of her new assignment with Sanford and no mention of her being in China herself. She began to believe that her idea that she was a decoy had some merit.

She sat on the bed and took out her address book. She found her aunt's number and made an international call from Shanghai to Beijing on her cell phone. She thought about using the hotel's phone, but she concluded the cell would be safer. When she reached her aunt, she was hit with a barrage of questions in between squeals of joy.

Without having the chance to ask, she found out that her parents had paid her aunt a visit and stayed for two days, and they had a wonderful time catching up. According to Aunt Ming, her parents were looking for a place on the outskirts of Beijing where the property values were cheaper. Mary told Aunt Ming that she would be coming to Beijing in a few days and that Aunt Ming should try to find her parents and get a contact number for them. She was pissed that her Dad was too cheap to buy a cell phone.

Mary wished Aunt Ming well and told her she would be seeing her soon. The call helped. That they were looking for a place to live confirmed that they were in China of their own free will. Mary started getting ready for bed when there was a knock on the door. Mary looked through the peephole and saw it was John Benson, a member of the Sanford team. She left the chain on and opened the door.

"Yes, what can I do for you, John?"

"Hi, I skipped the dinner with the guys and I was wondering if you'd want to have a drink or something?"

"No thanks. I'm just about to turn in. I didn't get much sleep last night."

"Are you sure? The better we know our partners, the better the working experience will be."

"I'm sure. Why don't you try Pat? Maybe she'd like a drink."

"We've had a drink before. Now it's your turn."

"I don't drink!" Mary slammed the door and John jumped backward, startled at the sound. He walked away muttering under his breath.

Mary got ready for bed while she organized her thoughts for the conversation she was going to have with

Charles in the morning. She looked at her watch and calculated that Eric should be having breakfast on the other side of the world. She dialed his number and got his voice mail. Still annoyed with John, she left a curt message, giving Eric an hour to return her call before the window of opportunity closed for another day.

Mary stretched out on the bed and read the hotel magazine while she waited for Eric's call. The room was on the twentieth floor and the view of the city was beautiful, so she left the drapes open. She fell asleep.

It was the morning sun that woke her just minutes before the hotel wake up call. She checked the clock. Since Eric hadn't called, she was going to have to make a special effort to stay calm all day. Every man in her life was disappointing her. She took a long shower.

That evening in Beijing, Hui Kai was being disciplined for not handling his charges in a professional manner, for not being aware that Mary was in China and for having led her to believe that her parents were being detained by the government. He knew that his communications were being monitored by his superiors. They knew that Mary would find out the truth of her parents' trip and determine that Hui Kai was not credible.

It was emphasized to Hui that handlers had to be viewed as being credible to their agents. It was emphasized just short of hospitalization. Hui was left with a renewed hatred for the agents in the field. His treatment also made him swear revenge on his superiors.

Hui knew he was responsible for only one small piece

of whatever plan his superiors had devised. He didn't even know the real objective. As far as he knew, he had completed his part. Mary Chang and Eric Wing were together, and Mary agreed to work with the CSA. Hui had done all that he was asked to do. He assumed that Mary was just a decoy. What did it matter that he didn't know that she was in China and he was trying to leverage her parents' trip to control her?

Hui was hurt, not only from his beating, but from the lack of appreciation for his work. He hated his superiors and his peers. He knew he was capable of so much more, but there was no chance to advance. If he did well, he was ignored. If he made a mistake, he was punished. He did enjoy being a handler and having control of agents in the field. He liked some of them and despised others. Mary was at the top of his 'Agents I Despise' list.

She was an amateur with no formal training, not really an agent at all. Hui knew it was a mistake for her to be chosen to join the Montgomery group and get close to Eric Wing. After seeing her briefly face-to-face, he hated her more. She didn't show him any respect and she didn't know her place, she was just like her father. She was a product of the West, and she was not to be trusted.

Hui nursed his injuries himself at home, a small apartment fifteen minutes from work. He looked around his small well-kept bedroom. It looked sterile to him just like his life and his wife. He suffered the pain from his bruises in silence. He didn't want his wife to know that he had been punished for poor performance. She had not lived up to her responsibility to give him a son, but she would not let him fail to live up to his. To preserve the peace and quiet in the household, he didn't share his failures with her. Since his successes were few and they were never acknowledged, he didn't share them either.

What conversation they had was limited to the weather, the rising cost of food, and the problems with their neighbors. Their marriage was over; they had no shared goals or dreams. They were roommates who occasionally had sex. After every miserable day at work, he had to come home to a small apartment, to a woman he no longer loved, who could not give him a son.

Despite the severity of his beating, Hui did not miss a day of work. His agents depended on him, the real ones. Even though Mary Chang was obviously a decoy, the pain in his side reminded him that he had to monitor and support her as if she were a real asset. He had to somehow apologize to Mary about misrepresenting the status of her parents in China. He would be happy if Mary Chang would suddenly disappear, never to be heard from again. He sat at his workstation and tried to compose a message for Agent Chang. Their strained working relationship had to be fixed and she had to be told that her parents were staying in China by choice.

It has been reported to me that your parents are not being detained here in Beijing. They are here of their own free will. It is unfortunate that there was a misunderstanding of your parents' status.

If the CSA has given you an assignment, I would like to know what it is. I understand your itinerary brings you to Beijing soon. I would like to meet you at your convenience when you get here.

Hui looked the message over. It was as apologetic as he was willing to be. He also tried to convey the impression that he was interested in any assignment that the CSA might give her. Finally, he wanted to make her think that she was important and respected. It irked him that he was almost asking permission to meet with her, but he hit 'send' and the message was on its way.

Mary had toast and coffee in her hotel room, rather than having to eat breakfast with the others. She turned on the computer in case Eric sent her an email, and she saw the message from Hui. She read it twice. It puzzled her; it had a polite tone that she wasn't used to. She recognized the change in interest about the CSA assignment. She turned off the machine and gathered her things for the meeting. She was lost in thought as she left the room and walked to the elevator.

It was not going to be a good day. Eric hadn't called or written, John was a jerk and her handler had undergone a personality change. Most disturbing was Hui's interest in her assignment for the CSA. She could visualize a scenario in which she had no credibility with either side. She was a pawn; she just had to go along, whichever way she was pulled.

She entered the meeting room and saw everyone from the Sanford team standing around making small talk, waiting for the Chinese restaurateurs to arrive. She walked up to John.

"John, you're a jerk. Don't ever try to come to my room again. Any dealings we have with each other will be strictly business. Do you understand?"

John stammered something and Mary turned and walked to the other side of the room. Everyone was shocked. Charles got everyone to take their seats. He reviewed the objectives for the meeting, as he glared at Mary. She returned his glare without blinking. The Chinese group came in the meeting room, apologizing for being late. The meeting began and the shocking confrontation between Mary and John was temporarily forgotten.

Charles avoided Mary until the meeting was over and they were alone in the room. His posture was stiff and he looked like he was desperately trying to control himself. She could see that he was furious.

"How dare you publicly confront a client like that?"

"Before you start on your tirade, I want you to know something. I am not a whore and I will not be treated like one. I was going to tell you and let you handle it, but I decided to take care of it myself. I don't want any misunderstanding. This job is not that important to me that I would degrade myself to keep it. I understand that you are upset with what I did, but you wanted a pretty face here. You should have told the client that I'm a valued member of the team and not a plaything. Now I can pack my things and catch the next flight home or you can apologize and assure me that this will never happen again."

Charles gritted his teeth and remembered the powerful friends who were looking out for Mary. He wanted to send her packing, but he had to know who or what he was up against when he finally got rid of her. "I'm sorry, it won't happen again." He turned and left the room. Mary felt that she had gotten what she asked for, but she wasn't sure.

It was 5:00 PM, too early to call Eric; she wanted to hear his voice. No, he was the one who needed to make the call. It had only been two days, but she missed him terribly. Then she remembered that he didn't go to the CSA debriefing with her and she became pissed at him all over again. She looked down at her wrist at the tennis bracelet he bought her and scoffed.

"No piece of jewelry was going to make up for that mistake."

She felt that she could use that event for years to come, to balance out any overwhelming feelings of love or joy associated with Mr. Eric Wing.

She took the elevator up to her room. She opened the door and found the message light on the telephone blinking. The message was from Pat, who congratulated her for putting John in his place, and invited her to have dinner together again. She called Pat's room and accepted the dinner invitation on the condition that there would be no conversation about 'John the jerk'.

Mary lay down on the bed and thought about her mother and father. What could she say to them? They had made the decision to leave her behind and move back to China. They knew she would never agree to leave San Francisco with them. It bothered her that they didn't wait for her assignment to end and tell her of their plans face to face. Mary hoped that one of them wasn't ill, forcing them to return to China sooner than they wanted to. She was afraid that she already knew how their reunion would end. In the end, she would go back home and they would already be home. Mary tried to imagine what life would be like without her parents' emotional support. All she would have would be Eric and he needed a lot of work.

Eric was getting a lot accomplished setting up Project Pinpoint. The budget and staffing requirements had been laid out and he had already met with the board and the military and started to develop schedule and profit projections. He had been working nearly nonstop for two days. He was upset about missing his window of opportunity to call Mary the day after she left. He was determined to call her today. He figured he'd call at 6:00 AM, which would be 10:00 PM Shanghai time.

He showered and shaved while he listened to the television news. He hadn't been paying much attention to his attire since Mary left. He picked out a shirt and tie that seemed to go together. Once he started working, he didn't know if or when he'd break for lunch, so he was eating big breakfasts. He finished eating and sat down on the sofa in front of the TV with a cup of tea. He watched the tube for a few minutes. When a commercial came on, he looked at the clock. He figured that she'd be going to bed at 10:00 PM and they could talk intimately. He did have a few disturbing thoughts about her not being alone at night there in Shanghai, but he pushed them aside.

At 6:00 AM, he made the call to her cell phone. The phone rang twice before she answered.

"Hello, who is this?"

"You know who this is. I'm the only one who should be calling you at this hour."

"And you're the one who should have been calling me yesterday at this time."

"I'm sorry, Baby. I have no excuse. But I want you to know that I had a lousy day because of it. I miss you. How is everything?"

"Things are okay, I miss you too. Are you taking care of yourself?"

"Sure, I'm good. Have you talked to your parents yet?"

"No, but I'm reasonably sure that I'll be able to find

them once I get to Beijing."

"Good. I hope everything goes well. I was expecting to get some emails with pictures of Shanghai."

"I decided that you should make first contact."

"First Contact! What are we, Aliens? I thought we were beyond ancient dating protocols."

"It does sound silly when you say it out loud. I'm sorry; I forget that we're in a serious relationship."

"I don't want you to forget that for a minute, especially when you're half a world away. What's it going to take to impress it on you?"

"It will take more than a tennis bracelet."

"Ouch! Okay we'll find a more appropriate piece of jewelry when you get back home, if you'll agree to marry me."

Mary was silent and she started to tear up.

"Mary, are you still there?"

"I'm here."

"Well, what do you think?"

"I think we should be having this conversation face to face when I get home. Preferably, as soon as possible after I get home, maybe in the airport. Maybe I'll hop a plane tonight. No, I take it back. I don't want to wait. I want to hear a direct question right now."

"Will you marry me?"

"Yes!"

"I love you, sweetheart."

"Okay, I have to go to bed now. We'll talk again tomorrow. I have some screaming to do now. Goodbye, my love."

"Goodnight." Eric signed off, as he felt all the air go out of his body in one big exhale. He hadn't planned to propose; it just happened. There wasn't a doubt in his mind that he was going to do it eventually, but he had planned to wait until he was sure that she'd say yes. This was great. It was done. He sat quietly for a minute and regained his strength. He wanted to put his arms around her. The hard part was over. She belonged to him now. It would be clear sailing from now on.

Mary buried her face in her pillow and she screamed until her throat started to hurt. She lay back and looked at the ceiling through blurry, tear-filled eyes. She took a few deep breaths and began to relax. She wanted to call her mother and tell her the news, but she couldn't. Her joy subsided when she remembered that her parents wouldn't be in San Francisco for the wedding and her mother wouldn't be around to help her with her marital problems or to show her how to take care of the babies. She hoped that she could convince them to come home and share in these special events in her life.

Her mood changed again as she thought about Eric making a long distance proposal. She felt robbed. She wanted to look at the fear in his eyes when he asked her. She wanted to see him squirm as he knelt down on one knee. She'd make him propose again when she got home, but there'd be no fear or squirming, the suspense wouldn't be there. She thought for a minute and a smile exploded on her face and she shouted. "Mrs. Eric Wing!"

In the San Francisco Office of the CSA, Agent Morris was receiving a long distance call.

"This is Agent Morris, how can I help you?"

"Good morning, Joe, this is Ron. This trip has been a waste of time so far."

"Good morning, Ron, but I guess it's night time where you are."

"Yes, it is. I thought I'd give you a call and fill you in on our girl."

"I expected to get a written report, not a phone call."

"You'll get your report, this is an added bonus. As I was saying, the young lady is as straight as an arrow. She goes to her meeting, eats in the hotel and goes back to her room. She's made no direct contacts, just one cell phone call to an aunt in Beijing. Apparently, she's trying to track down her parents."

"Why did you call if you've got nothing to say?"

"She got an interesting incoming call."

"From who? About what?"

"From the boyfriend. He just proposed to her and she accepted."

"Oh shit."

"Yeah, I thought you'd be interested. Now if you have to eliminate her, the boyfriend will raise hell and tell the world that she was working for you. Even if you make it look like an accident, he'll probably cause trouble."

"All right, thanks for the call. Keep a close eye on her, there's still an outside chance she's on the level and she can live a long, healthy life."

"I'll be talking to you."

Morris found Coleman and filled him in on the phone

call.

"What are you thinking? Do you want to take out the girl and the boyfriend if she's dirty?" asked Coleman.

"We're authorized to eliminate commercial terrorists, not innocent citizens."

"I see the point of getting rid of those guys. They steal billions from our economy and there doesn't seem to be any other way of stopping them, but the girl? She's not big enough to matter."

"She's playing a rough game of double agent; the stakes are high. The orders are, if she's dirty, she's gone. It's as simple as that."

When he wasn't working, Hui Kai spent his time planning to get rid of Agent Chang. He wanted to discredit her to the CSA and have them eliminate her. If his plan worked, they would put her in prison for espionage and throw away the key. Hui also devised a backup plan. Agent Chang could have an accident in the streets of Beijing. The backup plan was risky, even an accident might appear suspicious to Hui's superiors.

Over the years, Hui had made connections with people who were in a position to use the information and material that Hui's agents obtained. Not all of the acquisitions his agents made were of interest to Hui's superiors, but his connections could make use of them and in turn, Hui would accept a reasonable remuneration. One of the connections, Qiang Chung, was a successful businessman who replicated and sold DVDs and designer clothing, as well as electronic items. Mr. Chung also had a reputation for being able to arrange accidents.

Hui was on good terms with Mr. Chung and was going to use one of his idle factories to meet with Agent Chang when she came to Beijing. It was a sinister looking place that was going to be used to help expose her to the real world of espionage. At the meeting, Hui would find a way to compromise Mary's assignment. If he couldn't compromise her assignment, he'd let Mr. Chung arrange an accident.

Hui didn't anticipate any trouble. She was an amateur. He paused and thought about how his life was going to be so much better without having to deal with the little American bitch. He grimaced when he thought about apologizing to her and taking a beating because of her. He hoped she'd die in prolonged, agonizing pain. His muscles tensed and his body twitched with rage as he thought about her. The sound of someone's phone ringing down the hall snapped Hui out of his thought induced trance. He was still trembling with hate and he struggled to calm himself. He relaxed, looked at the calendar and smiled. *"Just one more day until she arrives in Beijing."*

CHAPTER FOURTEEN

Mary slept on and off during the night, but she still woke up happy and full of energy. This was her last day in Shanghai and she wanted to get it over and move on to Beijing. Her real focus was to get home to Eric as soon as she could. The meetings in Beijing were scheduled to last three days. Then she'd find her parents, make her pitch to get them to go back home, or at least get them to promise to visit her.

She turned on the news and went to take her shower as she hummed the "Wedding March". She dressed and put on her makeup, still humming her new favorite tune. She pulled out her suitcase and packed. Everyone was going to check out and bring their suitcases to the meeting room and take off for the airport after the meeting. Mary looked around the room to make sure nothing was left behind. She hadn't packed her computer. Before putting it away, she turned it on. She held her breath until she saw that there were no messages. She packed her computer and hummed her way to the elevator.

As usual, the last day of the meeting was a waste of time; all the important decisions had already been made. Charles and the Sanford team were patting themselves on the back about how smoothly the meetings went. Mary's confrontation with John was long forgotten. The day seemed to drag on and on, then it was finally over and everyone grabbed their bags and headed for the hotel airport shuttles.

The flight from Shanghai to Beijing was two and a half hours, about 665 miles. They went from hotel to hotel in five hours. They left Shanghai at 4:00 PM and it was just after nine when Mary was escorted into her room by a smiling, eager bellhop. She stretched out on the bed and saw the blinking light on the phone. She picked up the phone and dialed the front desk to retrieve the message. She was told that a car would be sent for her at 10:00 PM and return her to the hotel at 10:45 PM. She was to bring her work materials with her.

She hadn't thought about the flash drive since it was given to her on the bus. She was going to meet Mr. Chin and exchange flash drives. She got the drive from her vanity case and put it in her coat pocket.

At 9:55, Mary put on her coat and went down to the lobby. She walked out of the front door and saw a car waiting. She opened the door and said, "I'm ..."

"Get in Miss Chang," said a voice from the back seat. She looked in and saw Hui Kai seated comfortably. She sat next to him.

"I thought you said that we were going to meet at my convenience."

Hui clenched his teeth and said, "I'm sorry, it couldn't be helped. We need to talk before you have any contact with the CSA here in Beijing."

"What do you want?"

"Please be patient; we'll talk when we reach the meeting place."

They drove for about fifteen minutes to an industrial area and stopped next to a side door of a factory building. Hui opened the door for her and they went inside. They entered a dimly lit entry hall and walked to a dingy office that looked like a fire trap with papers and boxes piled in the corners. There was a desk and two chairs in the center of the room.

"Have a seat."

"If we're not going to be long, I'd prefer to stand."

Hui tried hard to control himself in the face of her arrogance. "What assignment did the CSA give you?"

"They gave me a flash drive to exchange with one of their agents here in Beijing."

"Let me have it."

Mary reached in her pocket and handed it to him. Hui would have slapped her if she had tried to give him a hard time. He took it and went to the desk and opened a drawer and took out a netbook computer. He plugged in the drive and downloaded its contents. He handed the drive back to Mary.

"What's that you got?"

Both Mary and Hui turned, startled by the sound of the voice. Hui instinctively reached in his pocket, but he had no weapon.

"Take it easy, relax." Qiang Chung stepped into the light.

"What are you doing here?" asked Hui.

"It's my place, isn't it? I came to see what you were up to."

"This doesn't concern you."

"Everything that goes on in my place concerns me. Aren't you going to introduce me to the young lady?"

"No, I'm not; we were just leaving."

Mary was frozen with fear. The surroundings and the situation scared her, but even more frightening was the fact that she recognized Chung from one of the pictures that the

CSA had shown her during her debriefing. She stood perfectly still and said nothing.

"Chung, if you want to continue our association, you'll leave now."

"All right, all right, I'll go. I just want you to know that I'm interested in everything you do, and I'm aware of almost everything you're into. You're right; it wouldn't look good if your employer found out about our association. I'll say goodnight." Chung walked out of the office and they could hear him leave the building.

"I'm sorry about that, he…"

"Sorry? You idiot, if the CSA finds out that I met with you, I'm finished." Mary was livid.

"Take it easy, Chung doesn't want anyone to see us together and he doesn't even know who you are."

"All the same, this was a bad idea."

"No harm done, I'll take you back to your hotel now."

Outside the factory across the street, two men watched Chung leave and get in his car. One of the watchers started the engine and began to follow Chung's car from a safe distance. The passenger dialed a number on his cell phone.

"Good morning, this is…"

"I know who it is. Our girl is on the move. She left the hotel and was driven to a factory south of the city. We waited outside for a few minutes and guess who came out?"

"Let's do this without the guessing games," said Morris.

"Okay, Number Four came out and drove way."

"Number Four!"

"You're damn right, we're following him now."

"What about the girl?"

"Forget the girl. Do you think I should have stayed and waited for her?"

"No, you're right, Number Four is the priority. Stay with him."

"If we get an opportunity to play with him, we will."

'If you don't get an opportunity, make one. On your next call to me, I want to hear that he's had fun."

"I'll be talking to you soon."

Number Four, Qiang Chung, had no known address. He had a number of real estate holdings throughout China. He rarely appeared in public and he was sought after by several government agencies, domestic and foreign. Since he had friends that were bought and paid for in his own government, he was somewhat protected. He was responsible for producing and selling millions of dollars of counterfeit merchandise. Qiang Chung was a major commercial terrorist.

Chung was followed to an upscale residential area, to a large house on about a half acre of land. It was covered with trees and shrubs almost obscuring the house. There were no guards visible. The agents parked two houses away from Chung's and waited. It was 11:07 PM. The street was not well lit and most of the houses on the street were dark. Ron and his partner, Li, made themselves comfortable while they watched the house. Li flipped a switch above his head to prevent the dome light from coming on when the car door was opened.

At 2:15 AM, they got out of the car and opened the trunk. Side by side, they opened gym bags and took out hoods and night vision glasses, which they put on. The glasses were small, state of the art devices, that were activated automatically when they were put on. The agents put on multi-pocketed vests and gloves, then quickly moved toward the house. There was no external security. Chung wouldn't call the police even if there were a break-in. He spent most of his time trying to avoid the police. His security system was to move from safe house to safe house unnoticed. Li picked the lock on the back door. Ron found the main power switch in the garage and he flipped it to the off position.

Searching the house for Chung was not as difficult as the agents expected. They passed through the kitchen and they heard Chung snoring upstairs in the master bedroom. They climbed the stairs and looked in the room and saw him on the bed with a half empty bottle of rye near his pillow. They positioned themselves on either side of him. First Li slipped his gloved hand under the pillow to see if Chung had a weapon within reach. Then Ron opened a packet and pulled out a small saturated piece of cloth and placed it gently over Chung's nose. Chung didn't react. After a few seconds, his breathing became labored and he weakly tried to swipe at his nose as if an insect was on it. The agents grabbed his arms and Ron pressed the cloth to Chung's nose. He was too weak to resist.

Li went to the bathroom and started filling the bathtub. While he waited for the tub to fill, Ron searched the room for any information about Chung's operation. Ron and Li took off Chung's pajamas and carried him to the tub and placed him in. They let his head slip below the surface of the water while he was still able to breathe. Li folded the pajamas neatly while Ron put the liquor bottle on the nightstand. Before leaving, they searched the rest of the house. They found nothing. Chung kept the details of his operation in his head. Without him, his business would be severely disrupted. The agents restored the power and exited the house. Back at the car they repacked their gear and drove north toward the city. It was 2:57 AM, 10:57 AM San Francisco time. Ron dialed a number he knew by heart.

"Hello, this is…"

"The list has been reduced by one." Ron ended the call and turned to Li.

"Do you know where we can get something to eat at this time of morning?"

Agent Morris in San Francisco got the message; Number Four, Qiang Chung was dead. He greeted the news with mixed emotions. He was glad that the wet team in Beijing had done their job successfully, but his double agent, Mary Chang, led them to the target. She was dirty and they had to get rid of her. Morris thought for a minute and he realized that he had to wait. Maybe Ms. Chang could lead his agents to other targets. She needed to be left alone to go wherever she wished, and she needed to be kept safe, at least temporarily.

Morris still had his phone in his hand and he pressed and held down the number 8.

"Ron, your day's not over yet. Go back to the factory and check on the young lady."

"No need, I got a call when we were following Chung. My man at the hotel said she was delivered back there at 10:55 PM last night."

"Good, keep watching her. Dirty or not, she may turn out to be our best asset."

"Will do, right after we get some sleep."

Mary woke up at 7:04 AM. She had a restless night and she was still shaken from meeting face to face with one of the men that the CSA was after. It didn't help that she still had to meet with Mr. Chin and give him the flash drive, but she had finally made it to Beijing.

Mary called her aunt. It had been four days since they last spoke, so there had to be some news of her parents' whereabouts. She let the phone ring, but no one answered. She hung up and went to take a shower, planning to call again later. The water was hot and it helped her relax and think. She dried off and put on a pair of jeans and a tee shirt. It was Saturday and she and Pat planned to shop and sightsee all weekend unless Mr. Chin sent for her.

She was about to call room service for breakfast. She thought for a minute and she pulled out her address book to check for any other relatives in or near Beijing. There were none. Her cell phone started ringing.

"Hello, Sweetheart."

"Oh Eric, I'm glad you called. I miss you so much."

"I miss you too. Your trip is half over; just a week or so more and you'll be back in my arms. I can't wait. There are so many things I want to do with you. I don't know what we're going to do first."

"I don't have that problem; I know exactly what we're going to do. We're going jewelry shopping."

Eric laughed. "You're right of course, but don't forget that I'm not a rich man."

"That doesn't matter as long as you spend your money like one." They both laughed. "How are you doing? How's that project of yours coming along?"

"You know I can't talk about it, especially not with you."

"I know, I know. I just want to know that you'll have time for me when I get back home."

"I'll make time for you. Have you talked to your parents yet?"

"No, I haven't found them yet, but I just got here. I'll find them when I'm done with these meetings. Work always gets in the way of what's important."

"You'll find them. But if you have trouble, you might want to contact your CSA friends. I wouldn't be surprised if they were tracking them. The CSA considers them foreign agents, don't they?"

"They did at one time. Maybe you're right. I'll call Agent Morris. But let's change the subject for a moment. Once we're married, it would be nice if you worked on projects that weren't top secret and of no interest to foreign governments. I'd like our talks around the breakfast table to be open and honest."

"I'll see what I can do. Hey, about the big day, do you want a long engagement or not?"

"That depends on whether or not I can convince my parents to come back to San Francisco for the wedding. If they agree to attend the wedding, then we'll wait and plan something big. If they won't come, there'll be no reason to wait. You'll be my only family."

"I know having your folks there will make you happy, but I don't want to wait. If it were left up to me, we'd get married right away. And if they agreed to come, we'd get married again when they showed up."

"I think we've talked long enough. You're going to

make me cry."

"Did I say something wrong?"

"No, my darling, just the opposite. I love you."

They talked for a few more minutes, and then Mary hung up and stretched out on the bed. She was happy in spite of all her problems. The last two phone calls with Eric had changed her life, or would soon change her life. Now, Eric was the most important person in her life. As long as she had him, nothing else mattered. She'd miss her parents, but they made their choice to move to China and they were happy with that choice. She'd find a way to end this craziness with the CSA and the Chinese and concentrate on being the best wife she could be.

Hui Kai was at home watching the late news broadcast, when he learned of the accidental death of the criminal, Qiang Chung. The reports of the accident were preliminary, but the deceased was found by his cleaning lady, apparently drowned in his bathtub after spending the night drinking heavily.

Hui would have expected Chung to die by being shot by a rival or the police. An accidental death seemed suspicious. It was more likely that he died violently and the government altered the facts for the general public. Hui planned to tap his sources in Beijing Municipal Public Security to find out the details of Chung's death. But, regardless of how he died, he was a valued associate and now Hui would have to find another buyer for the intelligence he had to sell.

Hui knew about Qiang Chung's business. He knew that even though Chung had vast holdings and a lot of people working for him, he kept everything in his head. He had no second in command as far as Hui knew. Chung was afraid of being killed and replaced.

Hui had an idea, a good idea. He would replace Chung and take over his businesses, at least the ones he knew about. At the office, Hui had a file on Chung that he had created over the years of working with him. It contained a history of all transactions he had with Chung and all of Chung's holdings that he or his agents were able to find.

Hui made sure his wife was asleep and he left the apartment and drove to the factory where he and Mary were the night before. He still had the key that Chung had loaned him. He entered the dingy hallway and passed the door to the office that was last night's meeting place and walked onto the factory floor. He looked around the large open area. The factory hadn't been used in months. There was a door at the far end of the factory floor. He tried it, but it was locked. He kicked it with no effect. He tried the key and the door opened. There were no windows in the room, so he turned on the light. This was what he was looking for, Chung's actual office. There was a neat desk with a large, comfortable looking desk chair, wooden cabinets and carpeting.

Hui went quickly behind the desk and tried to open the drawers. They were locked. He went back out on the factory floor and found a metal rod. He went back to the office and started working on the drawers. After a few minutes, he was able to pry them open and he started rummaging through them. He found bank statements and checkbooks for eight different people. He found contracts and receipts for equipment purchases. Among the papers were monthly bills for water and power for ten different properties. There were twenty-two credit cards and an old tattered book held together by an elastic band. He opened it. He wasn't sure but it looked like Chung's business ledger. If it was authentic, it had everything he needed. Chung didn't keep everything in his head after all.

Hui looked at his watch, it was after 6 AM. He had been going through Chung's documents for hours. He knew that there were more secrets to discover, but he had to get home before his wife missed him. He packed up most of the important items he found and straightened the office and locked the door behind him.

On the way home, it hit him that he was already a millionaire. With the checks and credit cards that he had taken, he could empty all of Chung's accounts. He had to pull over and catch his breath and relax for a minute. He got home and put his newfound fortune in his tool box in a closet. He was able to slip into bed without waking his wife. He was always curious as to how his wife could do nothing all day and still sleep like a log at night.

He was able to rest for forty-five minutes before he had to get ready for work. He didn't close his eyes. He couldn't sleep anyway. He needed time to figure it all out. He'd take over the whole operation. Most of Chung's employees didn't know who they worked for, so it would be business as usual for them. Hui got up and completed his morning ritual. He put the ledger and a checkbook in his satchel and went to work. He wasn't thinking and he nearly kissed his wife goodbye before he caught himself. He knew that he had to be careful not to do anything unusual.

Hui went through the motions at work, but his focus was on his new enterprise. He was still formulating his plan, but it included working out of the factory. Chung had his office there so it had to be safe. Hui would pay all the bills that came in, to make it look like business as usual. He would discreetly visit all of Chung's properties and find out which counterfeit items were being made where, and meet the people Chung had working for him. Hui decided that there was no need to transfer money out of Chung's accounts. If he needed money, he could simply write himself a check. Taking over the operation was going to take time, but Hui Kai was a patient man.

Mary made it through her first and second days of meetings in Beijing and she was thrilled that everything was going smoothly. If everything proceeded as planned, the last day's meeting would just be a formality. Then she could concentrate on finding her parents.

Back in her hotel room, she remembered what Eric had said to her about having the CSA help her find her mom and dad. She thought to herself, "*Why not?*" She found Morris' card and dialed the number. The phone rang three times before she realized that it was 4 AM in San Francisco. She was about to hang up, then decided to leave a message.

"Hello, who is this?"

"Oh, Agent Morris, I'm so sorry. I forgot about the time difference. I thought I was calling your office number."

"My calls are forwarded to me wherever I am. What do you want? Did something happen?"

"No, no, nothing happened. I was hoping you could help me."

"Help you how?"

"I need to find my parents while I'm here in Beijing and I was hoping that you could help."

"Oh, for Christ's sake, how could I help you?"

"I'm sure someone in your agency is interested in their movements. I'm hoping someone is having them followed. If that's true, you can find out where they are."

"Nobody here cares about your parents. They've been out of the game for a long time. Nobody's tracking them."

"That's too bad, because here's the way things are. Something did happen here. I've got some information for you, but I'm not coming home until I find my parents. Either you help me, or be prepared for a long wait until our next debriefing."

"All right, I'll ask around, but I'm not promising anything."

"Thank you, Agent Morris, goodbye."

"Yeah, right." Morris hung up, but he hadn't finished talking. "It's going to be a pleasure to give the order to get rid of that bitch." He looked at the clock, 4:08 AM. He was wide-awake now. He wondered if she really had anything to tell him. He couldn't take a chance. It wouldn't hurt to ask if anyone was watching the Changs in Beijing.

Mary hung up, smiling. She mentally checked off another item on her to-do list. She prayed that her little grandstand play with Agent Morris would lead to locating her parents. The sooner she saw her parents, the sooner she'd be back with Eric. She hoped that she hadn't oversold her debriefing to Morris. She was sure he'd want to know that she saw one of the men in Morris' pictures.

She'd wait two hours before calling Eric. She wanted to make sure he got enough sleep. She planned to keep him awake a lot when she got home. She checked her computer for messages. There were none. It appeared that her handler had other things on his mind besides her.

By 10 AM, Joe Morris felt like he had worked an entire day. Four cups of coffee hadn't helped enough. He talked to his boss about Mary Chang's request, and his boss queried the Active Operations Data Base. The Changs were not connected with any active operation. Morris was glad he was not going to be able to help Mary; he didn't like being blackmailed. He didn't really think that she had anything important to tell him; after all, she was dirty.

He checked his watch; it was 10:15 AM, or 2:15 AM Beijing time. There was a sixteen hour time difference. He read the report about Qiang Chung's death written by a man with firsthand knowledge of the event. Everything looked good; the authorities ruled the death accidental. What was disturbing was that the loss of Chung didn't seem to have any effect on his businesses. It had only been a few days but nothing had changed.

Morris sent an email to his associate in Beijing to continue monitoring Chung's businesses. If they didn't start to fail, he was to look for a new name to add to the hit list. He worked until it was time for lunch and he and Coleman were in the mood for Italian, so they took off. At 1 PM, when they returned, Morris called Mary. The phone rang four times before she picked up.

"Who is … Hello?"

"Ms. Chang, this is Agent Morris. Sorry to call so early, but I thought you'd want to know right away."

"What is it, did you find my parents?"

"No, unfortunately I was right, the agency has no interest in your parents, and we're not tracking them."

"Thank you, Agent Morris, I appreciate your promptness. I won't forget it."

Morris chuckled and hung up. Mary was beginning to hate Morris, but she did want to know whether or not the CSA could help. Once again, she was on her own. It was 5:10 AM and there was no point trying to get back to sleep; she never could fall back to sleep once she was awakened.

She sat up in bed when she realized that she had another source in Beijing. She got up and turned on her computer. She sent a message to Hui telling him that she had to find her parents before she could return home. She didn't know if he could or would help, but she thought it was worth a try. She turned off the computer and turned on the TV and went to take her morning shower.

Refreshed from the shower, she dressed and watched the news until it was time for breakfast. She ate in the hotel restaurant while reading the morning newspaper. In the back of her mind was the thought that she wouldn't be able to complete her assignment and pass the flash drive to Mr. Chin. She had it in her pocket in case he made contact. She hoped meeting with him wouldn't interfere with her search for her folks. It was time for the meeting to begin and she walked quickly to conference room B.

CHAPTER FIFTEEN

It was almost 6 PM in San Francisco and Agent Morris had arranged to have a meeting with VP Eric Wing in his office at Universal. Morris didn't want the meeting, but he decided that he had to inform Wing of the agency plans for Mary Chang. Wing had to know that she was working against the interests of the government.

When he arrived at Wing's office, there was no one in the outer office, so he knocked on the door and walked in. Wing was seated behind the desk and he stood to greet him.

"Sorry to barge in, but there was no one outside."

"Yes, my secretary has gone for the day. Have a seat."

"Thank you. I need to talk to you about a delicate matter and an important one. Your fiancée has been seen in China meeting with a known terrorist."

"Does that surprise you? She is working for you, to find out about the bad guys, isn't she?"

"Yes, but we believe she is actually working for the other side."

"What's your proof?"

"The contact we just mentioned for one thing. During her debriefing, we showed her a picture of that individual and she said she'd never seen him before, but on her first night in Beijing they were seen together. When she returns to the states, we are going to have to deal with her."

"You mean you're going to arrest her based on one sighting with a bad guy. I don't think you have enough evidence to make a case against her."

"We're not going to arrest her, we will detain her."

"For how long?"

"Indefinitely."

"Excuse me! What country is this? You are going to detain an American citizen based on almost nothing? I don't think so."

"Because of your close relationship with Ms. Chang, we wanted to extend you the courtesy of letting you know what was happening."

"What makes you think you can get away with holding her without due process."

"Read the Patriot Act, we can do a lot in the name of national security."

"Do you know what I can do? After years of working on military projects and making government contacts, I can call any one of six Congressmen or four Senators whose numbers I have in my cell phone and put you and your agency in a shit storm that you wouldn't believe."

"Now that's not necessary, I just wanted to give you a heads up..."

"If anything happens to Ms. Chang, I mean anything; you won't know what hit you."

"I'll leave now; I think I've said all I have to say."

"Before you go, I want to say that I'm pleased that you're on such good terms with Mary that she confided in you and told you that we're engaged. She and I were the only ones who knew. I hope you're not abusing the Patriot Act with illegal wire taps."

"Goodnight, Sir." Morris left and firmly closed the door behind him.

Eric was shaking with anger. Before this, he hadn't realized the real danger involved with what Mary was doing. She wasn't a trained agent, just homeschooled. He couldn't understand why the CSA was taking her activities so seriously. He knew he had to warn her, and he also knew the CSA would probably be listening.

Eric called the hotel, but he couldn't get through. She wasn't in her room and there were instructions that the meeting was not to be interrupted. He left a message that she should return his call as soon as possible. He didn't care that her return call might be monitored; he had to talk to her.

He hung up and paced back and forth, and then he picked up his cell phone and searched for a number. He actually only had the numbers for three Congressmen and one Senator and he was going to give them all a heads-up about the potential fallout from the activity of a rogue government agency, the CSA.

Hui was at work early and he got Mary's message as soon as he came in. Work was much more enjoyable now since much of the time was spent working for himself. Taking over the factory operations was easier than Hui had thought it would be. Qiang Chung had everything automated. The amount deposited in each of the five operating checking accounts dictated the amounts that would be deposited into each factory boss' account, and they in turn were responsible for paying the factory workers. The amounts deposited in the remaining three income accounts were pure profit.

He had visited one factory and introduced himself as Mr. Chung's representative. He was able to get the details of the factory operation and told the factory boss that he would provide new product prototypes and managerial support. No one questioned him. Chung had conditioned his people to keep their mouths shut and to do what they were told.

Life was getting better for Hui. The previous evening, he had made love to his wife for the first time in months. The enthusiasm with which Hui performed the act shocked Mrs. Kai, who was already surprised at being touched in the first place. Her normally sour disposition changed temporarily the next morning and she couldn't think of anything to criticize before he left for work.

The one problem Hui had was money. He had it, but he couldn't spend it, not lavishly like he wanted to. He couldn't buy a new car without raising suspicions. All he could do was make small prudent purchases. His wife complained about the toaster so he was able to buy her a new one. She complained about the dishwasher so he was going to have it replaced. His wife was becoming more human, and he had to satisfy himself with an improving marriage and the small purchases he could get away with.

He thought about the consequences of getting caught for making counterfeit merchandise. It was a crime, but in China everyone did it. Counterfeit goods were sold openly in the city. The scale of the operation would be the problem. If caught and convicted, he would be imprisoned for at least ten years. Hui knew that he had to be disciplined and hide his wealth.

Hui had almost forgotten about Mary. He was happy to do anything that would expedite her return to San Francisco and her demise at the hands of her countrymen.

Hui had gotten a report that the Changs were staying in a small hotel in the Eastern section of the city while they waited for their house to become available. Hui replied to Mary's message and got back to his primary interest.

The last day of the Beijing meetings was the longest. It didn't help that absolutely nothing was being accomplished. All the major agreements and decisions were made on day two. Mary couldn't wait to get out and start her search. Finally, all the goodbyes had been said, and everyone else was on their way to the airport.

Mary kept the room since she didn't know how long she would have to stay in Beijing and she didn't want to impose on Aunt Ming. She went to the room and changed her clothes quickly. Usually, it took days for the handler to reply to her messages, but she turned on her computer to check, just in case.

Your parents are staying at the Beijing Templeside Deluxe Hotel, No. 2 Bai Ta Xiang, Zhao Deng Yu Road, Xicheng District.

Mary stared at the message and she squealed and covered her mouth before someone in a neighboring room called hotel security. She wrote down the address, grabbed her coat and ran out of the room, ignoring the message light on her phone. She had the doorman hail a taxi and she was on her way. Twenty minutes later, she was walking up the steps of a small house. There was a sign in the front of the building, but it didn't look like any hotel she had ever seen. It looked more like a bed and breakfast. She was directed to one of the eight rooms in the hotel and she knocked on the door, to be greeted by her father. She almost knocked him over as she ran into his arms. Her mother, on the other side of the room, let out a yell and hurried to share the embrace of her daughter.

Everyone was crying and talking until Mary's father tried to quiet the women and restore order. "Why are you here? You had a long term assignment, is it over?"

"No, but nothing has been compromised. I had to see you."

"Why, what has happened?"

Mary told them that she had fallen in love and was going to get married. She said that she was afraid that she had lost them and wanted them to always be a part of her life. Her father went to the window and looked outside and spotted a car in the middle of the block with two men sitting in the front seat. He opened his suitcase and took out his camera. He shot three pictures of the men and the car. He shook his head and grabbed Mary, forcing her to sit down in a small wooden chair. He sat on the bed and pulled the chair close to him.

"Tell me everything!"

Mary was shocked by his attitude and the rough way he handled her.

"I don't understand, I …"

"Tell me everything! What are you working on? Who are you working with? Tell me everything that's happened since you left home three months ago."

The look in his eyes told Mary to do what he asked and not to hold back anything. She told him every detail of her activities. It took her twenty-five minutes, and he listened and didn't interrupt her with questions.

When she was done, he put his head in his hands and

said nothing. Her mother, who had also been listening quietly, began to cry. Mary had a perplexed look. She reached over and touched her father's knee.

"Daddy, what's wrong?"

"They're going to kill you."

"What! Who's going to kill me? Why?"

"The Americans are going to kill you and our people set you up."

"I don't understand. What are you talking about?"

"Your little assignment, deliver a flash drive to an agent here. There probably is no agent, but that doesn't matter. What does matter is they can tell if the flash drive has been accessed. When you pass it on or return it to the agent in San Francisco, they'll have proof that you can't be trusted and they will eliminate you. On top of that, your handler knew what he was doing when he accessed the drive and gave it back to you. He was setting you up."

"Why would my handler set me up, I've done everything he asked of me."

"Did you do everything with humility and respect?"

"You think he'd kill me because he doesn't like me?"

"I should have stopped this years ago. I worked with Hui Kai for a short time before I retired. He tried to convince me to stay, but I wouldn't. Then he asked if I would let you run a few errands for him, and now you're in this mess."

"Is he doing this because you left?"

"I don't know. The handlers operate independently. Each agent they recruit or receive increases their status. Each one they lose decreases it."

"But Eric and I are still together like he wanted."

"Yes, but he may have decided that you're more trouble than you're worth, or that you may make a mistake. It could be any one of a hundred reasons that he wants to get rid of you, and that's what he's done."

"What can I do?"

"You can stay here with us and we can go into hiding, or you can go back home and tell them all you know."

"I have to go home; my life is there with Eric."

"Mary, you're a spy. You shouldn't be, but you are. You can't trust anyone, not even Eric. You have to be careful."

"I love Eric and I trust him."

"Go home if you must. I still have friends and sources who can help me find out more about your handler."

Mary and her parents talked for hours about her situation and her options. She decided to spend the remainder of the week with her family before heading home. They visited with all the relatives in the area that she didn't know about and Mary was able to forget her troubles temporarily. She called Eric to introduce her parents to him and he told her what she already knew, that there would be an unhealthy reception waiting for her at home. She told him that she was coming home anyway.

Simon Chang knew the immediate threat to his daughter was from the Americans, but there was nothing he could do about it yet. He spent his time contacting his former associates to learn what he could about Hui Kai. There were four people that Chang talked to about Hui. The conversations were long and pleasant and they brought back memories of many useful years working for the Chinese Government. One of his contacts was able to provide Simon the information he was looking for. Simon learned that Hui Kai was quietly taking over the operations belonging to the late Qiang Chung.

Simon remembered what his daughter had told him about the meeting with Hui and searched the internet and found the newspaper coverage of the death of Qiang Chung with his picture. He showed the picture to Mary and she identified him as the man at the factory.

"Good," said Simon. "Give me your cell phone and the number of your CSA contact."

He looked out of the window at the men in the car who had returned for a second day. He dialed the number.

"This is Agent Morris, how can I help you?"

"Agent Morris, this is Simon Chang. My daughter tells me that you know of me."

"Yes, I know you."

"I'm just learning about you, sir."

"Really, what have you learned so far?"

"I've learned that you've got at least one team doing wet work here in Mainland China."

Just then the car across the street started and sped away. And the phone was silent.

"Agent Morris, are you still there?"

"Yes, I'm here."

"Agent Morris, I'm a trained agent, my daughter isn't. She's an innocent and I'm told that you've targeted her for termination. That would be a mistake. If anything happened to her, the real story about the death of Qiang Chung would come to light. And that would be very embarrassing for your country."

"You don't have any proof."

"I just have the real toxicology report and a picture of your hit team. It's not conclusive, I admit, but it will make it impossible for you to continue operating here. So nothing had better happen to my daughter and she is no longer in your employ. Do we understand each other?"

"Yes."

"Good, and for your information, her handler set her up so that you would eliminate her. So, I have one more task to perform. Goodbye, Agent Morris."

"Goodbye, Mr. Chang."

Simon sat back in his chair and let himself relax. He got away with his bluff about the toxicology report and Mary was going to be safe from the Americans. He didn't hate the Americans; they were only doing their jobs. But when he thought about Hui who wanted to kill a young girl for no reason, his chest swelled with anger and he fought to control his hand tremors.

As he sat motionless in the chair, he found that he had enjoyed his conversation with the American agent. Aside from the real threat to his daughter, the entire experience made him feel alive. He thought about Hui and his first impulse was to have him killed.

Hui was playing a dangerous game. Unlike his predecessor, Qiang Chung, Hui was out in the open where he could easily be found and disposed of. Hui had bosses who wouldn't approve of his side businesses. Hui also had inherited Qiang Chung's competitors who would love to get rid of him. Simon decided not to move on Hui. He would wait and deal with him after consulting with his associates.

Before Mary left to return home, Simon told her that she would no longer be working for the CSA and she would probably not be hearing from Hui Kai again. He also told her that circumstances would not permit him to return to the US and that she and Eric should come to China at least once a year. The airport send-off was emotional. Aunt Ming and her family were there to say goodbye. Mary cried for an hour after the plane took off.

In San Francisco, Agent Morris was reading through the file on Simon Li Chang. Chang was suspected of operating as an agent for the Chinese in the United States for over twenty years. He was never caught and his assignments were unknown. There were several intervals of intense surveillance documented, but with no results. There was a kill order in late '92 which was rescinded when the Democrats returned to power. Later, after he retired, it was found out that Simon Chang was a skilled agent who was credited with turning more than a dozen assets, none of whom were ever brought to justice.

"Damn, he's got us. If he exposes any of our wet work teams, it could mean big trouble for the Agency."

Coleman was sitting on the edge of Morris' desk with a scowl. "Didn't he say that he had a copy of the real toxicology report? That means either the police or the government already knows that the death wasn't an accident."

"Yeah, but they don't know who might have done it. Chang can put that piece of the puzzle together for them."

"Okay, we're in a standoff. He keeps his mouth shut and his daughter stays alive. I think we're safe."

"I guess we are. But it still pisses me off that little asshole beat us."

"Get over it, he's retired. He only got involved because of his kid. He'll never bother us again."

"I'm not so sure. If the girl does any more spying, we'll go after the father first, and then we'll take out the girl."

"Why wait?"

"There's no point in inviting trouble. Don't forget about the boyfriend and his government connections."

"Right, let's hope it's over."

Morris closed the Chang file and put it in his out-bin to be returned to the file room.

Eric was in the office working, but accomplishing very little. He had spent the past two days worrying about Mary. It was a little past noon and she was scheduled to land at 11:15 PM. Eric was going to be as close to the gate as possible. He wasn't going to let her out of his sight. He was on his way to lunch when his cell phone rang.

"I hope you can hear me over the sound of the engines."

"Mary! How are you?"

"I'm fine and I'm on my way home."

"How did everything go with your parents?"

"They're fine, but they're not coming home for the wedding or to see any of our kids born. I promised them that we'd go see them at least once a year. I hope that's all right."

"Right now, I'll agree to anything. I called a few Congressmen about the CSA..."

"Don't worry, Dad said that it's all taken care of."

"But how?"

"I don't know, but Dad says it's done. This call is probably costing me a fortune. I should have called collect."

"That's very funny. Soon all our money will come out of the same pot."

"I'd better go. I love you."

"I love you too. I'll be there when you land. Bye."

Eric hung up relieved but skeptical. He wasn't going to take any chances. He still wasn't going to let her out of his sight.

Hui was getting used to his new position as kingpin, but his day job was suffering. And his young agent in San Francisco was about to have a CSA arranged fatal accident. Soon his criminal businesses would be running themselves and he could turn his full attention back to the business of industrial espionage. It was difficult to be concerned about handling agents after he estimated that the annual profits from counterfeiting handbags, jeans, DVDs and the rest of the items added up to over 20 million Yuan.

If he could manage to operate for one year, he'd be set for life. He had to be careful and he had to be smart. He made sure that the factory workers were well treated. He began diverting money from Chung's income accounts to his own private account. He also accumulated thousands of Yuan in cash in case he had to run and hide.

After a few short weeks, Hui had everything under control; all his business interests were operating successfully. His only concern was that the Americans had not eliminated Mary Chang. His informants in San Francisco had seen her continuing her life in the city. She was completely involved with Eric Wing. There were rumors that the two of them were planning a wedding. Hui tried to make contact with her, but she did not respond to him. He ordered his man in the bay area to give Mary a warning that she would be in trouble if she continued to ignore his messages.

Two weeks after the warning was delivered, Hui was on his way home after work and he had a chance meeting with Simon Chang. Hui invited Simon to his place for tea and the two old working associates chatted about old times.

"I was surprised to learn that you came home to Beijing after so many years. I thought you would stay in San Francisco with your daughter," said Hui.

"She was starting her own life and she didn't need us anymore. She got a good job with a company that did business in China, so we thought that we would see her from time to time. How have you been doing? Still handling agents, informants and couriers around the world?"

"Yes, I'm doing the same thing I've done for twenty-four years now. It was a surprise seeing you in this neighborhood. Are you looking for an apartment around here?"

"No, I really came here to see you. We've been watching you for a number of weeks, and gathering information. And since you have recently threatened my daughter, I thought it was time to talk to you."

"What are you talking about?"

"You know what I'm talking about. I am really curious.

Do you hate me so much that you would have my only daughter killed? What did I do to you?"

"It seems that you found me out. Okay, I'll admit it. I did hate you. You were the agent who got all the credit and all the glory. You were the one who Dr. Jiang Wang went to America to see personally. You were the one who knew it all. Of course I hated you. And your daughter was just like you. She didn't know her place. I believed that if I eliminated her, I'd destroy you."

"You're right, you would have. But now, you are the one in jeopardy."

"Me?"

"Yes, you are running a criminal enterprise and your superiors at the OBO won't like it when they find out, the authorities won't like it when they find out, and your competitors won't like it when they find out. It's a shame that you can only die once."

"Simon, please don't do anything. Don't tell anyone."

"You tried to kill my daughter."

"Please, I beg you. I'll do anything you ask."

"Hui Kai, over my strong objections it's already been decided that you will not be exposed if you do what you are told."

"What do I have to do?"

"You have to continue to operate Qiang Chung's factories. You also have to turn over ninety-eight per cent of the profits to us."

Ninety-eight percent?"

"That's right. You have the choice of getting two per cent or nothing."

"Who am I giving the money to?"

"We're a group of your old working associates. We are trained former agents who are familiar with criminals and criminal behavior. It would be a good idea to accept our terms and to keep them."

"Ninety-eight percent?"

"Personally, I hope you decline our offer. I would prefer to see you die. Whether or not you agree with our terms, if you make another move on my daughter, I'll make you wish you were never born. I have to be going now. Thank you for the tea. We'll talk again soon."

Simon put on his coat and left. Hui was too stunned to move. His dreams of wealth were being taken away and there was nothing he could do about it. He lowered his head and he wept.

A car was waiting for Simon when he stepped outside. The driver opened the door and closed it after Simon settled into the back seat.

"Were there any problems, Sir?"

"None to speak of."

The car turned southwest toward the Feng Tai district. They drove for twenty minutes. They pulled up to a well-kept house. Simon got out and the driver pulled away. Once inside, a young woman took his hat and coat. He walked to the living room where his wife, Chi Mei, was sitting reading a book.

"What happened?"

"I gave Mr. Kai our proposal. Now he's thinking it over. I don't see that he has a choice, but I could be wrong. He'll need to be watched."

"He tried to kill my daughter. I want him dead."

"I know, I know. Right now he's useful to us. If that changes, then we'll deal with him."

"I'm sorry we ever left San Francisco; now I'll only see Mary maybe once a year."

"You shouldn't complain. Your daughter was a hippie working as a waitress on the wharf. Now she's a well-paid professional woman. Before, she had no man in her life but me. Now she is engaged to a nice young man that I handpicked myself, who happens to be the Vice President of a major company."

"You neglected to mention how you almost got her killed with your little game of cloak and dagger."

"True, I didn't think that idiot Hui Kai would be so vengeful. When Jiang Wang visited us in San Francisco, he said that he had Hui under control."

"Ha! Dr. Jiang Wang is as bad as all the rest. He's only interested in stealing American secrets. You say my girl is safe now. What happens when Dr. Wang wants the next piece of technology from your handpicked son-in-law? Mary will try to protect her man and Hui or someone like him will be in her life again."

"Calm down. Don't get excited over something that will never happen. Pinpoint is a short-term project. When it's completed, Eric will be managing the move to China again. I have Charles Tong already talking to the board at Universal Technology. It will just be a matter of time before your daughter, her husband and whatever babies they have will be moving to China permanently. Maybe then you'll give me some credit for carefully planning our move home."

###

In this first novel, *The Unreported Crime,* Robert C. Stewart's main character is seventeen year old Juan Santos, who wants to be a police detective, but cannot afford to study full-time to reach his goal. Juan works with his father on the night shift as a janitor cleaning a local police station and uses his natural abilities and insight to help two less than talented detectives solve crimes. In the course of their investigations, Juan helps them to discover an unreported crime and a corrupt member of the department, while inadvertently placing himself in danger. This intriguing adventure will keep you guessing until its unpredictable ending.

www.ingramcontent.com/pod-product-compliance
Lightning Source LLC
Chambersburg PA
CBHW061142170626
46809CB00003B/959